It was pitch black inside... until a strange, green fluorescent light crept into the corners. The light shone through the holes illuminating them. All at once, Robyn saw rows of skulls, leering at her, grinning between chipped, brown teeth. Everywhere she looked she could see them. Row upon row of menacing skulls. And now she could hear footsteps, running...

"Grab her!" a voice shouted.

The footsteps came closer. Robyn desperately looked for a way out but every hole was blocked by a skull. Right in front of her, the monstrous mouth of one of the skulls began to yawn, a gaping chasm so wide Robyn thought its jaw would drop off. But it just kept widening and the skull seemed to grow with it. Robyn shivered. The footsteps sounded so close now, her pursuers must be almost upon her.

Taking a deep breath she took the only exit she could see – into the cavernous mouth of the skull. Its jaw snapped shut and Robyn was trapped, left in darkness, but at least alone. Then a disembodied voice began to call her name...

First published in 1997 by Usborne Publishing Ltd, Usborne House, 83-85 Saffron Hill, London EC1N 8RT, England.

First published in America March 1998

U.E.

ISBN   0 7460 2460 6   (paperback)
ISBN   0 7460 2461 4   (hardback)

Typeset in Times
Printed in Great Britain

Series Editor: Gaby Waters
Editor: Phil Roxbee Cox
Designer: Lucy Parris
Cover illustration: Luis Rey
Maps: John Lawrence

SKULL ISLAND

Lesley Sims

CONTENTS

1

PARADISE

"You're going *where*?" cried Robyn Curtis's best friend Melissa, when Robyn told her the news at break-time.

"Paradise!" Robyn grinned.

"I thought that's what you said." Melissa looked amazed.

"It's a tropical island," Robyn explained.

"You lucky thing," said Melissa enviously. She paused to fish an apple out of her bag. "How come you're going there?"

"It's my mother," Robyn said. "You know she's just started her own public relations company?"

"How could I forget?" Melissa said wryly. Mrs. Curtis had agonized for months over whether to set up her own business, and most of the agonizing had been done on Melissa's mother's sofa.

"Well, she's just been given her first job... by Gerry Sylvester!"

Melissa was impressed. Everyone knew Gerry Sylvester and his *Global Green* corporation. They had stores all over the world, selling everything from Aboriginal panpipes to bedsocks from China. '*People not Profit!*' their slogan ran. '*We put the Environment First!*'

"He's bought an island called Paradise and built this whole luxury complex on it," Robyn continued.

"That doesn't sound like putting the environment first to me," said Melissa.

"That's why he's hired my mother. It's all been done without spoiling the island and it'll be her job to let people know that. Eco... eco-tourism, I think she called it. She says it's a brilliant idea."

"So what does your mother have to do exactly?" Melissa asked.

Robyn looked blank. "I'm not sure," she admitted. She only had a hazy idea of what public relations involved. "I expect she'll do lots of stuff to advertise the place. You know, like writing a glossy brochure about the island and the hotel."

"And you get to go too," said Melissa. "You're so lucky. I wish my mother did something interesting like that." But before she could say more, the bell for the end of break rang and they went back to their classes.

When they met up after school, Melissa was more subdued. "We were going to do so much together this summer – build our tree house, go ice-skating, see some new movies..." she said as they began to walk home. "I don't suppose you can fit me in your suitcase?"

"I would if I could," said Robyn. "I'll probably be stuck on my own all day while my mother's working..."

"It'll be fantastic," Melissa interrupted. "There's bound to be lots of things to do, like... well... swimming and stuff." Melissa paused. What did people do on tropical islands? "I expect lots of postcards telling me all about it!" They had reached Melissa's house.

"I'll write to you every other day," Robyn promised.

"Only every other day?" Melissa teased.

"Well, there's only so much you can say about lying in the sun, swimming and generally having a good time," said Robyn, with a grin.

2

EDEN

Three weeks later, Robyn and her mother were on the last leg of their journey to Paradise, aboard a small private plane. One of Gerry Sylvester's staff, a tall, thin man with a sun tan, had met them off their jet, whizzed them through the airport and onto the little plane, which was emblazoned with the words *Global Green*. His badge said he was *Rick. Personal Assistant*. Robyn had never met anyone less personal.

He'd been polite and businesslike, but somehow not at all friendly, and the only time he addressed Robyn, he'd called her 'little girl'. You can imagine how she felt about him after that. He now sat across the aisle from them, his face impassive. But what Robyn found really irritating was the fact that he was wearing his sunglasses *inside* the plane.

"I don't think much of Mr. Sunglasses," Robyn

whispered to her mother. "I suppose he thinks it looks cool."

Mrs. Curtis smiled. "I saw the look you gave him when he called you *little girl*."

Robyn glanced around. All the other passengers were grown up. None of them looked as if they were on their way to a tropical island. They had grim, bored faces to match their grim, boring, work clothes – suits and sensible shoes. At least her mother had made an effort with white jeans and a bright jacket.

"All right?" Mrs. Curtis asked, squeezing Robyn's hand. "I do hope you enjoy yourself, but I don't know how much time we'll have together."

"Don't worry," Robyn reassured her. "I'll have a great time." She sat back in her seat and looked through the tinted glass window. Way below them, the sea was a deep, shimmering turquoise, clear enough to make out the dark shapes of rocks lurking beneath. It glittered in the sun, lazy waves rippling its surface.

In the distance, but growing closer every second, was a large green island, fringed with white and set in the vast blue sea. A continuous stretch of sand skirted the island, cast with the long shadows of exotic palms.

"We'll shortly be arriving in Paradise," Rick announced, as the plane began its descent. Robyn watched enthralled as distant blue and yellow dots became wooden houses and vibrant splashes of orange and red blossomed into flowers. The plane was approaching a landing strip set in a clearing, but there didn't seem to be any airport buildings beside it.

"According to Gerry's office, not a single tree was

cut down to make room for the runway," Robyn's mother told her. "That's exactly the kind of concern for the environment I'll want to highlight."

"Oh," said Robyn, only half-listening. They had finally arrived! With engines roaring, the *Global Green* plane touched down and slowed to a halt.

As the door of the plane opened, Robyn was struck by the fiercely bright sunlight. The heat wrapped itself around her, warm and damp. It was like suddenly being submerged in a heated swimming pool. "Where's the airport?" she asked, looking around in surprise.

"There isn't one," said Rick, who was standing behind her. "Gerry doesn't put up unnecessary buildings. Make your way down please," he added curtly. "You're keeping everyone waiting."

At the bottom of the steps stood a tall, smiling figure, familiar from countless television interviews. He was wearing a loose *Global Green* T-shirt and cotton shorts, and there was a relaxed air about him. Robyn recognized him at once: Gerry Sylvester.

"Hi," he said, as she reached the bottom of the steps. "You must be Robyn. I just wanted to say a quick hello to you and your mother before you head off to the resort." He nodded in the direction of a gleaming, luxury minibus with the *Global Green* logo on the side.

Before Robyn could reply, her mother joined her. "Great to meet you again, Julia," Gerry Sylvester beamed, shaking her hand.

"Likewise, Gerry," said Mrs. Curtis, in a tone that Robyn thought of as her 'business voice'.

"Well, there's a busy schedule ahead of you," Gerry

told her. "But we'll talk later. You must be tired."

It was then that Robyn saw a motorcycle parked beside the landing strip. Gerry Sylvester climbed onto it, smiling. "Electric powered," he explained. "No exhaust fumes. We don't have pollution in Paradise!" With that, he gave a final wave and drove off.

Meanwhile, everyone else had climbed aboard the minibus, and the last of their luggage had been transferred from the plane. When Robyn stepped into the air conditioned bus, it felt like walking into a fridge. After the heat outside, it was deliciously cool. She and her mother took the only spare seats, right at the back.

The *Global Green* minibus followed the broad sweep of the coastline around the island. The sea looked so inviting, Robyn wanted to jump in there and then. But there were two whole weeks ahead of her for swimming... maybe she could learn to snorkel, or even try some scuba diving. The possibilities seemed endless.

The minibus bumped along a narrow, dusty track which gave way to a wider one, then almost at once they were in a market. Robyn was overwhelmed by the vividness of it all. Women sat by the roadside on boxes, or behind gaudy stalls, great pyramids of ripe, shiny fruit and vegetables piled before them. An old woman in a yellow dress sat staring into the distance. She noticed Robyn watching her through the window and gave her a toothless smile.

Barefoot children ran among the stalls, dodging the mounds of green bananas which lay everywhere. "This looks wonderful," said one of the other passengers, in a strident voice which carried the length of the bus. "I hope we get to try some local produce."

"At the resort, everything that *can* be grown or bought locally *is*," Rick told the passengers, his eyes still hidden. "That's the *Global Green* way."

Robyn wondered if he wore his sunglasses in the bath or even in bed. She grinned at the thought. Soon they had left the market behind and were driving along a road lined with trees. Flowers bloomed by the road, their spiky petals waving the bus on as it swept past.

A few minutes later, they turned into a long, smooth drive, pulling up outside an imposing white building. It had a porch supported by columns, and numerous balconies, each one decorated with sweeps and swirls of ironwork. On one side of the steps stood a rusty cannon; on the other, an old-fashioned iron lamppost. Robyn had never seen anything like it.

She waited impatiently while the other passengers, talking in low voices and gathering their hand luggage, trooped down from the minibus. They began to follow Rick up the steps to the grand entrance. Last off the bus, Robyn paused to read a plaque.

EDEN RESORT
THE GOVERNOR'S MANSION
FOR TOURISTS WHO CARE
Global Green Corp.

Robyn raced after her mother and arrived, breathless, in a spacious hall with potted palms and a whirring fan on the ceiling. Rick was introducing a small, neat man in a crisp, white shirt, "... and this is Gilbert Hope, Manager of Eden."

"Thank you, Rick," the man beamed to the dozen or so tourists. "Once you've signed the register, you'll be shown to your cabins. There's an informal reception with Gerry Sylvester, and a chance to meet the other guests, on the veranda of the Bamboo Terrace this evening at six."

Cabins? thought Robyn, imagining a log cabin. She'd thought this was a luxury hotel. Porters in *Global Green* T-shirts were bringing in the luggage from the minibus, but Rick carried Robyn and her mother's suitcases personally. "Gerry asked me to look after you," he said. "Follow me."

They entered a corridor lined with portraits, mostly of stern-faced men and women sitting ramrod upright. One caught Robyn's eye. It was of a girl about her age, wearing an old-fashioned dress, with her hair in ringlets. She, too, sat up straight, her hands resting demurely in her lap, but the painter had captured a mischievous glint in her eye. *Flora Marriott, 1764*, Robyn read as she went by.

Rick led them outside, through a shady garden bursting with flowers, and stopped in front of a large wooden building thatched with palm leaves. "Your cabin," he said. "And here are your keys, though you'll find you can safely leave it unlocked. One set for you, Mrs. Curtis, and one for your..." Robyn held her breath, "daughter," he continued. "We have two restaurants in Eden, or you can order Room Service. The fridges are stocked daily with fresh local produce and a selection of drinks, including our own filtered mineral water. Your cabin, like everything in the resort, runs on solar power."

He turned to Robyn. "The Eden complex isn't intended for children, so please respect the other guests' privacy and don't run around being noisy."

Robyn felt her cheeks redden with indignation. She glared at Rick but couldn't see past the blank stare of his sunglasses. How old did he think she was?

Rick left their suitcases just inside the door. "I'll leave you to unpack," he said to Mrs. Curtis. With that he was gone.

"Don't put Mr. Sunglasses in the brochure," Robyn muttered. "He's enough to put anyone off."

Mrs. Curtis smiled. "He's not very friendly, is he?" she said, opening the cabin. "Come on. Let's explore!"

"They call this a *cabin*?" said Robyn, in disbelief, as she wandered through the rooms. She'd never seen anything less like a cabin. It was almost as big as their house at home – bright and airy, with smart wooden furniture and well polished floors, with rugs in bold, geometric patterns. Constantly spinning ceiling fans kept it cool.

"It's lovely!" said Mrs. Curtis, walking out onto the large wooden veranda. "We can eat outside."

"There's even a Jacuzzi!" Robyn said. "And two bedrooms! Can I have the one overlooking the sea?"

"Of course you can." Her mother smiled and disappeared into the smaller bedroom to unpack.

Inside her room, Robyn flung open the window

shutters and realized why they were there. The heat outside felt almost stifling compared to the shady coolness of her room. She closed them quickly and looked around. On the bedside table she saw some sheets of paper stapled together and began to read.

Dear Guest,

Welcome to Paradise!

It is a particular pleasure to welcome you to this, the first season of the Eden Resort. There is no glossy brochure to tell you about its splendid facilities as yet. No, I'm hoping that you, my inaugural guests, will assist in its creation. I want Eden to be a resort which grows, adapting to the caring visitor's needs. So, once you have participated in the unique Eden experience, please tell me all your thoughts, suggestions and comments, good and bad.

What do you really like to know about a resort? Which service or facility do you particularly enjoy? Is there anything you don't like? Let's hope not!

It is only through listening to you, our discerning guests, that Eden will evolve into a true 'Paradise' and something we can all be really proud of.

Should you have any questions about Eden, please dial 'O' on your cabin telephone where our receptionist will be only too happy to help.

Attached is a brief history of the island and a map.

Enjoy your stay!

Gerry Sylvester, *Global Green Corp.*

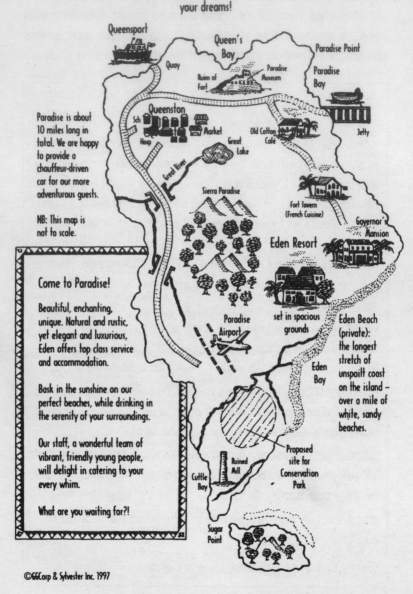

PARADISE ISLAND
The island of
your dreams!

Queensport

Quay

Queen's Bay

Paradise Point

Ruins of Fort

Paradise Museum

Paradise Bay

Sch

Queenston

Old Cotton Café

Jetty

Hosp

Market

Great Lake

Paradise is about 10 miles long in total. We are happy to provide a chauffeur-driven car for our more adventurous guests.

NB: This map is not to scale.

Great River

Sierra Paradise

Fort Tavern (French Cuisine)

Governor's Mansion

Eden Resort

Come to Paradise!

Beautiful, enchanting, unique. Natural and rustic, yet elegant and luxurious, Eden offers top class service and accommodation.

Bask in the sunshine on our perfect beaches, while drinking in the serenity of your surroundings.

Our staff, a wonderful team of vibrant, friendly young people, will delight in catering to your every whim.

What are you waiting for?!

Paradise Airport

set in spacious grounds

Eden Bay

Eden Beach (private): the longest stretch of unspoilt coast on the island – over a mile of white, sandy beaches.

Proposed site for Conservation Park

Cuttle Bay

Ruined Mill

Sugar Point

A Short History of Paradise

by K. Phipps (MA Westward Univ.) & C. Benjamin

Paradise Island lies eleven degrees north of the equator. Just ten miles long and less than five miles wide, it is one of the smaller of the Westward Islands.

The original inhabitants were Amerindians who lived in small settlements along the coast. The first European settlers arrived after the island was 'discovered' by Juan Paradiso in 1547. By the end of the 17th century, the island was under British rule and sugar plantations were being cultivated. Slaves from West Africa were imported to work on the land and in the sugar mills, and the island was soon a most profitable colony.

In the mid 18th century, New Paradise became the official home of the Governor of the Westward Islands. At this time, there were seven estates on the island, the richest of these being Sugar Point in the south. Although the acreage was relatively small, the first estate owners grew fabulously wealthy, leading to speculation of involvement in less legitimate enterprises such as unlicensed rum production and trading activities possibly linked with piracy. The magnificent Governor's Mansion was built in 1765. It is still standing and has recently been fully restored, now forming part of the new Eden Resort.

The plantations continued to thrive after the abolition of slavery and there was still a prosperous sugar industry in the early years of this century. Then, in September 1923, a devastating hurricane wiped out the entire sugar crop and the island sank into poverty. Today, with a population of just over 10,000, the hope is to revive the economy by welcoming tourists for the first time.

Robyn yawned as she turned the page. Then two words caught her eye...

Skull Island

This tiny island was once a place of mystery and magic. Originally used as a burial ground by the Amerindian islanders, it remained sacred for centuries. It was rarely visited, as it was believed to be haunted by the spirits of the dead, and those brave few who did venture there returned with terrifying tales of evil spirits and skulls on spikes. Even today it is regarded with awe and, some would say, fear. More recently, there have been suggestions that its magical reputation was exploited by those with a more mercenary interest and that the island was used as a base for piracy, although this has never been confirmed.

The only volcanic island in the Westward group, Skull Island lies just off the south coast of Paradise and is home to some rare and endangered species of wildlife, including the leatherback turtle. It currently belongs to the Westward Islands' government and is a protected wildlife sanctuary which is closed to the general public. Those with a legitimate interest, such as for research purposes, may apply for a visitor's permit, although these are strictly limited.

Skull Island, thought Robyn... what a wonderful, spooky name. She opened the shutters again. The sun was setting rapidly and her room was full of shadows and the perfumed scent of flowers. Looking out to sea, in the distance, she thought she could see the brooding outline of land above the water. Could that be Skull Island?

3

CAUTIOUS

Robyn strolled, sleepy-eyed, out of her bedroom the next morning, to see a figure walk onto the veranda, hidden behind a tray piled high with fruit.

"Morning!" a woman's voice cried cheerfully. "I'm Mary. Welcome to Paradise!" She put the tray onto the table as if it was no weight at all and wiped her hands on her apron, before holding a hand out to Robyn.

Robyn shook it. "I'm Robyn. My mother's here to do some work for Gerry Sylvester."

"A *special* guest of the boss? I shall have to mind my Ps and Qs," Mary laughed, whisking coffee, orange juice, muffins and a gargantuan bowl of fruit off the tray onto the table. "Enjoy!" she called, as she left.

"Thank you," said Robyn. She tried to peel and quarter a mango as she would an apple, but the stone was too big and the flesh stuck to it, like an unripe nectarine. She gave up and gnawed at it. Sticky juice ran down her chin and her tongue flicked out to catch it. She took another bite, thinking back to yesterday evening in the Bamboo Terrace and all those boring people sipping cocktails as they listened to Gerry Sylvester, still in T-shirt and shorts, giving his welcoming speech.

"Here on Paradise we work with the environment," he had begun enthusiastically. "Not against it, not despite it, but *with* it. We use only natural products, and, wherever possible, products from the island itself. For example, your cabins are built with wood from the local rainforest. This means that they blend in with local surroundings, the forest can be thinned to allow new growth, and local people benefit from the work it generates. This is a part of what is called biodiversity, which is a new word for an old belief – the belief that we need to balance the needs of the planet, animals and plantlife with our own..."

And so he had gone on for what felt like hours. His enthusiasm was incredible and it seemed to be infectious, even if Robyn couldn't get quite as excited about it as everyone else in the room.

Robyn was licking mango juice from her fingers, and wondering whether to have some pineapple, when her mother appeared.

"I overslept," Mrs. Curtis said, sounding flustered. "I forgot to reset my alarm clock. Why didn't you wake me?" She sat down groaning and poured herself some coffee. "Oh, I feel jet lagged. And what a late night...

Well, have you thought about what to do today?"

"I thought I'd look around Eden first, and see what the beach is like," Robyn said. "And can I have some money to buy a postcard for Melissa?"

"Take some from my purse over there," said her mother. "Oh, Rick was saying last night that the sea's not as safe as it looks, so please don't go swimming alone. Now, who am I meeting first this morning?"

Robyn decided not to ask her mother to peel a pineapple for her and took a banana instead. As she reached for one, to her amazement, two tiny birds with yellow breasts flew onto the table and began pecking at some sugar in a bowl.

Mrs. Curtis nearly dropped her coffee cup when she finally looked up and noticed them. Unperturbed, they continued pecking for a while, before flying off. This place is incredible, thought Robyn, stuffing the last of the banana into her mouth.

Her mother got up to leave. "See you back here for lunch," she said. "About twelve?"

Robyn nodded. "See you later," she muttered, through a mouthful of banana and set off to explore.

* * * * * * * * * *

It didn't take long to look around. The grounds were vast – but there was nothing in them except for flower beds filled with perfectly trimmed plants, and grass you couldn't walk on. Then there were places where she clearly wasn't supposed to go, like the Meditation Pool. It was nothing special, just a swimming pool made to look natural with the help of a few large rocks. It was full of people, floating about and humming. Rick happened to pass by as she was watching them. "Can't you read?" he glowered. "*Private* means not for little girls. They don't want to be stared at."

There was an ordinary swimming pool too, but Robyn didn't feel welcome there either. Walking past the tidy rows of wooden sunloungers, she recognized two people from the plane yesterday. They were stretched out, asleep in the sun. Behind them was a notice: *No diving, jumping or ball games*. A lone swimmer, wearing goggles, was making her way up and down the pool in determined straight lines.

Even the stretch of beach, sign-posted *Exclusively for the use of Eden's guests* seemed unreal. Not a footprint marred the white sand. Rick was right. Eden wasn't designed for kids. Everything was new and unbelievably neat. Not a single polished leaf on the potted plants looked out of place. If anything was out of place, it was Robyn.

She sat down on the spotless beach, letting a handful of sand trickle through her fingers. If only she could go in the sea. She felt disappointed. Of all the things she had imagined, she hadn't expected Paradise to be boring. She remembered how much fun the market had looked yesterday. Slowly, it dawned on her that perhaps it wasn't Paradise that was the problem – it was Eden.

Robyn decided that now was as good a time as any to write Melissa the first of her promised postcards. She stood up and wandered over to a little shop on the beach called The Natural Gift Shack.

It sold the sorts of things that beach shops always sell, only there were labels on everything, pointing out their 'eco-friendliness'. There were shell necklaces, biodegradable straw hats, aloe vera gel in recycled glass bottles and hand painted sarongs in subtle shades. There were also some postcards of local wildlife, not a great selection and all rather bent. Robyn bought one showing a leatherback turtle, sat down at a beach table and started to write...

Dear Mel,

This place is unreal. We have our own apartment a stone's throw from the beach. It's called a cabin, but you'd never guess from the inside. The bathroom has a Jacuzzi! The food's great and guess what? I've met Gerry Sylvester, the man himself! (He even knew my name!) I wish you were here though. Then we could explore together.

Robyn was signing off when she was interrupted by her mother.

"Hello, darling, I've been looking for you," Mrs. Curtis said. "We'll have to have a late lunch. I'm just off to a meeting with the Minister for Tourism. Gerry says the island's perfectly safe if you want to look around. There's a bus into the town which stops at the bottom of the drive. Do you have enough money?"

Robyn barely had time to reply before her mother was off again. As luck would have it, a bus pulled up as she reached the road. Robyn jumped on board. The bus was old and rusting, but painted in bright pink and yellow stripes and crowded with noisy passengers and animals. Robyn smiled. What a contrast to the deadly-dull beach.

They took the same route as yesterday in reverse. When the bus stopped at the market, most of the passengers got off. Robyn followed them. For a while she walked along aimlessly. Then she noticed a signpost pointing to the remains of a fort and followed it to an old brick building, overlooking the sea. The building was surrounded by rocks laid out in squares, which may once have been walls. Its wooden door, studded with iron, displayed a hand-painted notice:

PARADISE MUSEUM
Old Fort, Queen's Bay
ALL OF HISTORY IS HERE
COME ON IN! ENTRANCE **FREE**

The museum was full of a weird mish-mash of objects, from the everyday to the extraordinary. Squeezed in between a black umbrella, with the label 'Formerly the property of Preacher John' and a selection of spoons marked 'Spoons', was a bone marked 'Human shin 1.7 million years old.'

Robyn wandered around fascinated. Three teeth from an unknown mouth rested beside some broken pottery; a piece of weaving lay over a cast iron pot; and taking up the entire length of the room on one side, was a family sized canoe – minus paddles.

She wandered into a little back room filled with glass fronted cabinets. Here she noticed the name Skull

Island again, this time on a card beside some rocks:

HARDENED LAVA (pumice stone) from the last recorded eruption on *Skull Island* in 1578. Uninhabited even in ancient times, *Skull Island* was once used as a burial ground, hence its name. Until recently, it was believed to be haunted by the spirits of the dead.

Robyn turned away, coming face-to-face with the hollow sockets of a brightly painted skull. It was such a shock that she gasped. The skull was on a long pole but there was no card to say where it came from. She looked at it again and shuddered, before moving on quickly, accidentally bumping into a glass case.

Inside, mottled-brown with age, was a book. Half of its cover was missing but Robyn could still make out the faded words across the front: *The Private Journal of Flora Marriott, in the Year of our Lord 1765*.

"That was Governor Marriott's daughter," said a voice behind her.

Robyn jumped and spun around. She hadn't heard anyone else come in. But there stood a gnarled old man with dark, shiny cheeks and a yellow-toothed grin. The man held out a wavering arm. "Cautious Benjamin," he said, taking Robyn's hand and shaking it surprisingly firmly.

"Oh," Robyn replied uncertainly. It seemed an odd thing to say.

The man chuckled. "My name," he explained. "Yup, Cautious is my birth-certificate original name, for high days, holidays and any other day you care to mention."

Robyn smiled doubtfully. What was he talking about?

"I'm the curator here. Have been since the museum opened six months ago," he said proudly.

He lowered his voice and beckoned Robyn closer. "Anything to get away from my sister Patience and her constant nagging. But listen to me, rambling on and I don't even know who you are."

"Robyn," said Robyn. "Robyn Curtis. I'm staying at Eden with my mother."

"So, you enjoying Paradise then?" asked Cautious.

Robyn hesitated. "Yes," she said finally, in a slightly flat voice.

"Doesn't sound that way to me," said Cautious.

"Well, I wish my friend Melissa was here," Robyn admitted. "It's more fun doing things with other people."

"You want to talk to my friend Mary," Cautious told her. "She works for Mr. Sylvester. Her family's worked at the mansion since before I was born. Ask her to send her son Zack to keep you company. No, not him, he's the older one. Drat it, what's the youngster's name...?" He scratched his neck, a thoughtful expression on his face. "Interested in Flora Marriott's journal?" he asked suddenly.

"What?" said Robyn.

"The book in that case," Cautious said. "You might have seen her you know."

Robyn looked puzzled.

"Flora. There's a picture of her in the Governor's Mansion, brought over by her pa. Would you like to read the journal?"

"Can I?" said Robyn. "It looks very old."

Cautious chuckled. "Oh you can't have the original. But there's a typescript somewhere. Mr. Sylvester had a researcher from the university here to read it. Spent weeks working on it. Mr. Sylvester was very eager to have it done, for some reason. Friendly man, I liked him. Ken Phipps was his name. I helped him write a history of Paradise," he added abruptly. "Now, where did I put it?"

He shuffled off. Robyn continued looking around and came across some 'Amerindian knuckle dice'. She was just wondering what they were used for, when the man returned, carrying a messy pile of papers.

"That'll keep you busy for a while!" he said. "Ken changed the spellings, modernized 'em to make it easier to read. And he said some pages were missing, but he put in notes of his own to explain those. Well, anything else you want to know about Paradise, you just come and find me!"

Robyn thanked him and headed back to the market clutching the bundle of typed pages. It was incredibly hot and she suddenly felt tired, though it wasn't even midday. Maybe this is what jet lag feels like, she thought. Seeing a bench in the shade of a tree, she decided to sit down and read for a while, before exploring the town any further.

4

FLORA'S JOURNAL

April 2nd 1765

Father left today for New Paradise, to take up his appointment as Governor of the Westward Islands. As he departed, he gave me this wonderful leather notebook. I told him I would treasure it and use it to record all of my adventures, until we were together again.

I can picture him now, supervising the loading of his trunks onto the coach. For someone setting off on a grand adventure to a new world, he didn't look very excited. In fact, he looked positively bilious.

It was fortunate that I had with me some pills for just such a problem. The packet declared: 'Mr. Speediman's Patent Stomach Pills Guaranteed to Disperse Wind in a Most Surprising Manner.'

Well, it was those or leeches.

The house has been very quiet since his departure. Though he made little noise when he was home; he virtually lived in his study. The only times I heard him were when I slammed a door or whistled in the passageway. Then his shouts of, "Great heavens, Flora! Are you in a circus?" quite drowned out the cries of the mackerel and lavender sellers on the street.

Cook made hot spiced gingerbread for tea this evening to cheer us up. It wasn't much comfort and Biddy refused any, saying that she was a martyr to indigestion and all she wanted was a thin slice of plain white bread.

Yes, Biddy. She is my new governess and companion, hired by Father before he left. The name suits her, she is like a nervous, fussy mother hen. She has only been in the house for six hours and already Cook and I have lost all patience with her.

She is constantly whining and she has a large nose. Its size I suppose is hardly her fault, but what I cannot forgive (or forget) is the drip permanently swaying at the end of it. Ugh! If that were not enough, she is full of irritating sayings.

At supper I said I could not wait to join Father, I so long for excitement.

"Be careful what you wish for, it may very well come true," she snapped, tarter than a bag of windfall apples.

Why Father chose her of all people I will never know. He said I needed a steadying influence more than ever, now he was going away. I know that since Mama's death, he has worried that my manners are more those of a gentleman than a young lady, but to burden me with Biddy... I despair!

April 10th
Just think what I could have done, if only Father hadn't seen fit to hire Biddy. Yawning through our embroidery afternoons (the woman has a mania for handkerchiefs, which is extraordinary considering she never applies one to her own nose) I pass the time imagining the fun I could have had on my own.

April 15th
Biddy is proving a martyr to everything. It's a wonder she ever gets up at all.

[Pages for the remainder of April and most of May are unaccountably missing from the journal. It resumes with the entry for May 28th – Ken Phipps]

May 28th
No one ever had a more irritating governess. Some days I could scream at her for an hour without stopping. "Don't do this, Flora, don't do that. Is that wise dear? Time for your nap." Heaven preserve me!

June 3rd
Today I escaped. One whole precious day of freedom! Biddy was struck down with the vapours and had to keep to her bed.

Cook assured her I was busy with my silent piano practice, when in fact I had left the house at dawn, with a basket of sweetmeats, headed for Bartholomew

Fair. Father would have been horrified!

The streets were crowded with acrobats and hurdy gurdy players. I rode on a merry-go-round until my head spun, then reeled into a fortune teller's tent.

"You will shortly go on a journey," she promised. "But beware of the man with the pointed black beard. The way will diverge, choose your path carefully."

What nonsense fortune tellers speak! But perhaps Father will send for me soon.

June 9th

A letter from Father, dated May 5th. He has arrived safe and well and encloses a map of New Paradise!

'My dearest Flora,' he writes. 'I am well settled into the newly-constructed Governor's Mansion. The island is indeed spectacular, such plants and birds as you have neither seen nor could imagine.

'But to the purpose of my letter. I have arranged for you and Biddy to sail under the care of a Captain Humphrey Valentine. His cousin came here five years ago and is the foreman at the nearby sugar mill.

'Captain Valentine commands a small merchant ship called The Pelican, which is to depart from the city docks on June 12th, bound for New Paradise. You and Biddy are to be at the quayside no later than eight o'clock in the morning. I am trusting that everything will be arranged in time.

'That is all for now. I hope you are well and look forward to seeing you in two months or so.

'Wishing you a safe and speedy voyage,

Your loving Father.'

27

NEW PARADISE
from actual SURVEYS and OBSERVATIONS
by J. LAWRENCE,
GEOGRAPHER TO THE KING

37

Queen's Bay 13 26 16

Paradiso Bay 18   17

QUEEN'S BAY DIV'N   15

JAMES DIVISION   23

Fort James   14

Remains of a house in the Dutch taste

Where Juan Paradiso landed 1547

Great Lake

Man of War Bay

Old Cotton Tree

French fort abolished 1629

Great River

Paradise Mts.

MAN OF WAR DIV'N

18 7 8

15 Site of new mansion

10

Richmond Rogue, a small Rocky Island

EASTERN DIV'N

Very Uncertain Soundings and Rocky Bottom

HOG BAY DIV'N

GREAT RIVER DIV'N

The Water at the Mouth of this River is Very Unhealthy.

4   2

3   Jugus River

2   1

Fat Hog Bay 21 20

18 22 23

Some places not above a Fathom Water

19   14

5   7 13

SUGAR POINT DIV'N 15

2   4

Cutlass Bay

Between Skull Island & the Land it is very Foul Water & the Currents are very Strong and uncertain

OBSERVATIONS
Numerical Figures denote Depth of water in Fathoms & where Anchors are Exprefsed it is good Anchorage. Beware Richmond Rogue – so near the Shore that no prudent Seaman will come nigh it.

Sugar Point

New Paradise is Comprehended under 7 Divisions. Subdivided into 19 Plantations which contain in the whole 22,045 Acres.

SKULL ISLAND

I raced to the kitchen to tell Cook the good news. "The twelfth?" she shrieked. "In three days' time! How will we ever be ready? All hands to the pumps!"

June 12th

I cannot believe what I have done! I am bursting with it! But I shall start from the beginning. At six o'clock this morning, after a hasty wash and a slice of bread and jam, Biddy and I bid Cook a rather tearful farewell (the tears were Cook's) and boarded our carriage for the first stage of the journey.

Biddy did not utter one word in the carriage, though I was so excited I talked enough for both of us. But as I paused at the foot of The Pelican's gangplank, to let Biddy board first, she clutched my arm for a moment. Her face was deathly pale, her hands twisted in and out of each other and her entire body including her bony, drippy nose was shaking.

"I can't do it, Miss Flora! I can't!" she declared. She said she could not leave her home to go half way round the world, set upon by barbarous pirates as like as not or shipwrecked and left for dead on some uninhabited island. And then she said, her voice dropping to a whisper, that it wasn't proper being with all those men. No, she had decided, we would write to Father, to inform him of our decision to stay here.

I was furious. I had been waiting months for this day. Long, dull months with a feeble-minded, milk-pudding of a governess for company. Those stifling months with Biddy had wound me up tighter than a clockwork toy. The catch was about to be released.

29

As I fumed, a man appeared on deck. He wished us good morning, said that he was Captain Humphrey Valentine at our service and gave a pompous little bow. He came down the gangplank to welcome us aboard and I told him there had been a change of plan, that my governess did not feel able to join the ship. Biddy looked immensely relieved.

Captain Valentine told us he had no time to discuss it. There was a strong wind blowing and he wanted to make the most of it. He added that he dared not imagine Father's reaction to the decision but it was hers to make. He gave another little bow to Biddy, who blushed redder than his jacket.

"Yes, the journey is off," I said in a shaky voice. Biddy must have thought I was close to tears with disappointment for she murmured, "There, there, my dear, it's all for the best," and patted my hand consolingly. In truth, I was desperately trying to contain my excitement at the secret plan in my head. I snatched my hand away.

The Captain turned and walked back up the gangplank, calling, "Loose the moorings. Take up the plank, lads!"

Two men appeared, untied the mooring ropes on the quayside, then jumped up onto the ship and started to pull the rope attached to the gangplank. Biddy watched them, still dazed over her narrow escape. This was my chance!

I caught hold of my skirts and petticoats and leaped onto the gangplank just as it was lifting up off the quay. By some miracle I kept my balance and raced along it onto the deck. As I did, I thought I heard Biddy cry out, *"Oh, Miss Flora!"*

"You have spirit, girl!" Captain Valentine said admiringly.

I turned to wave goodbye to Biddy, only to see that she had fainted and even the smelling-salts of a concerned passer-by were failing to bring her round. It was then that I saw all of our bags piled up on the dockside next to her. I had just started a month-long voyage and all my worldly possessions were on the quay, barring this precious journal (which I keep with me at all times) and the clothes I stand up in.

But how many dresses will I need at sea? All that matters is that at last I am free from Biddy and on the brink of excitement and adventure!

5

SKULL ISLAND

The harsh beep of a horn broke into Robyn's thoughts and she looked up with a start. A driver was impatiently honking at the bus, which blocked the street as it picked people up.

The bus! Robyn glanced at her watch. The time had flown by while she was reading the journal. There was no time left to explore the town now. She scooted over to the bus, just before the driver closed the door.

She was dropped off at the bottom of the drive to the Eden Resort. As she neared the Governor's Mansion, she saw her mother coming down the steps, balancing papers.

"Robyn!" she called. "Ready for lunch? Did you have a good morning?"

"Great," said Robyn. "I found this weird museum. It's got a journal written by the girl whose picture's in the hall in the mansion. Can you believe it?" She remembered Cautious and smiled. "And I met the curator. He's got the funniest name. It's Cautious Benjamin, and he..."

She broke off. Her mother was nodding absently, obviously engrossed in the document which lay on the top of the pile.

"... he had green hair and he was taller than a house," Robyn finished.

"Really? That's nice," Mrs. Curtis said. She looked up, suddenly animated. "I've had a good morning too. Gerry Sylvester was telling me about his plans for a sanctuary for endangered animals. Did you know that the leatherback turtle is almost extinct?"

"Yes," said Robyn, who'd read it on the back of the postcard to Melissa.

"No," said her mother. "Neither did I. Gerry doesn't even plan to charge the public an entrance fee. That's a great selling point. 'There's more to life than money, Julia,' he told me." She smiled. "Part of Paradise Island will be strictly animals only. He doesn't want anything upsetting them."

Over a lightly spiced fish salad, Robyn's mother chatted on. She was brimming with ideas for the brochure she was writing and kept waving papers with different lettering under Robyn's nose.

"Which do you think looks better? Bold or italic for this? Black or silver here? Large type or small?"

Straight after lunch, Mrs. Curtis dashed off to another meeting. Robyn wandered out through the gardens. She walked past the main pool, and rows of sunbathers. Among them were the same two guests she'd seen that morning. They were still asleep, though they must have woken at some point, because they'd moved their loungers to follow the sun. Were they going to spend the entire day asleep?

Robyn strolled down to the deserted beach. Putting her hands in the pockets of her cut-off jeans, she walked along the wet sand where the sea met the shore, wondering what to do. If only Melissa could have come with her...

"Hey, you!" someone shouted.

Robyn looked around. A boy was striding in her direction, a fierce expression on his face.

"Er, me?" said Robyn doubtfully.

"Do you see anyone else on this beach?" the boy asked, rudely.

Robyn bristled.

"There's a reason for that," the boy went on, "This beach is private. It's only open to guests of the Eden Resort."

They were almost face to face. The boy stopped in front of her. But if he was trying to assert his authority, it didn't work – he was only half a head taller. Robyn guessed he was used to having the beach to himself. From what she'd seen, Gerry Sylvester's guests kept to the pools.

"But I *am* a guest of the Eden Resort," she said shortly. "I'm staying here with my mother, not that it's any of your business."

"Oh," said the boy airily, not looking in the least embarrassed. "Well, my mother works for Gerry

Sylvester."

"So does mine," Robyn said back.

"Oh?" The boy seemed genuinely surprised. "What does she do?"

"Publicity stuff," said Robyn, telling him about Curtis Publicity. "What about yours?"

"My mother's Mary," he said, as if that explained everything. "In charge of catering," he added. "You know, you don't look like an Eden guest," he went on, in a friendlier voice.

Robyn smiled. "No way! I'm not asleep, for one thing. Can you imagine coming to a great place like this and spending the whole time with your eyes shut?"

The boy's face relaxed into a grin and he nodded. "How long have you been here?"

"Since yesterday," said Robyn.

"I'm Ben," the boy said.

"Robyn," said Robyn.

"So how long are you here for?" Ben asked.

"Two weeks," Robyn answered.

"I could show you around if you want," said Ben, off-handedly.

"OK," Robyn said. "I don't mind being on my own you know, but it might start getting boring... Yes, OK."

Ben scuffed his shoes in the sand. "Er, where would you like to go?"

Robyn pulled a face. "How do I know?" she said. "I've only just arrived."

"Good point," said Ben. "Want something to drink?" He pointed to the far end of the beach. "My friend runs the Snack Shack."

Robyn nodded. They began to walk down the beach. Robyn looked up at the clear blue sky, then out to sea at an island in the distance.

"What's that?" she asked, pointing to it.

"Skull Island," said Ben. "It's a wildlife sanctuary. My brother Zack's the warden."

"Does he live there?" asked Robyn, intrigued.

"No, stupid," Ben laughed and shook his head. "No one lives there – only animals."

"What about all the spirits of the dead?" said Robyn, remembering what she'd read.

"Zack doesn't believe in any of that," said Ben. "My gran does though. She says it's a place of dark magic."

Robyn screwed up her eyes in the sunlight. It didn't look very magical. From what she could see, Skull Island was mostly covered in bushes and trees.

"It's full of skulls and bones, you know," Ben continued. "They're buried all over the island."

"What, even now?" said Robyn.

"Yes," Ben nodded. "And weird things used to happen there."

"Such as?"

"Well, a long time ago," Ben began, "hundreds of slaves were sent over there by one of the plantation owners. Hardly any of them came back and those that did were half crazy, telling terrible tales all about dead men's bones and a dark underworld deep beneath the ground."

"What were the slaves doing there?" asked Robyn.

"No one knows," Ben said. "There are other stories too. Boats used to disappear on the reef around the

36

island and were never found, not even the wreckage. Then there were sailors who put ashore by mistake and saw a ring of skulls on spikes and heard the rocks talking to them, or maybe they were voices coming from *inside* the rocks. Gran says what did they expect, going near sacred ground? She says the spirits were wreaking vengeance on them and the sailors brought it on themselves."

"Ergh!" Robyn said, remembering the garishly painted skull at the museum. "And your brother's happy to work there?"

"Of course," said Ben. "Zack doesn't believe in spirits. But he says the black magic stuff's been a good thing in a strange way."

"How come?" said Robyn.

"It keeps people away. And that's what has let the wildlife flourish," Ben explained. "Zack only goes to Skull Island every so often, because even *his* visits might disturb the balance of things. And whenever he goes over there, Gran makes sure he takes her most powerful charms with him!"

By now, they had reached a boarded-up hut. There was no sign of anyone else on the beach. "Is this the shack?" asked Robyn.

"Yup," said Ben. "Must have closed early." He looked at his watch. "It's getting late, I've got to go. See you tomorrow maybe."

6

THE JOURNEY BEGINS

A fter supper with her mother, Robyn sat out on the veranda. Moonlight was shining on the sea, and floating up from Gerry's Bar on the beach, came the murmuring voices and clinking glasses of Eden's guests. Mrs. Curtis had gone down to join them, muttering something about 'ambience' and 'the full Eden experience', whatever they were.

Robyn finished her orange juice and returned to the copy of the journal. She'd left it where Flora had jumped onto *The Pelican* just as it was setting sail, leaving her governess in a faint on the quayside. How exciting!

12th June
The port was soon a vanishing speck behind us. With a strong wind filling the sails and wheeling gulls

overhead, I could taste adventure in the salt spray on my lips. I swear if I had lifted my arms I could have flown, soaring past the birds and beyond the horizon.

The voice of the Captain barking at someone brought me back to earth.

What had I done? For a second my heart quailed. Then Biddy's voice rang through my head.

"Flora dear, always look before you leap." My spirits rose. Nothing could be as dreadful as her!

There are only five crew members and they were civil enough as Captain Valentine introduced me. All but one, a bearded giant, who snarled that women had no place at sea, that everyone knew it brought bad luck, and what did their fool of a captain think he was doing? But he said it so that only a bare-footed boy and I heard. The boy gave me a sympathetic smile. His name is Harry Joseph and he is the cabin boy.

As I write this, the fortune teller's words come back to me. The ill-tempered giant has a bushy ginger beard covering half of his face. I shall keep my distance anyway, so far as is possible on such a small ship, or 'brig.' (I think that is the word the bosun used.) The Pelican has just two masts. Square sails on top capture the wind, sending her scudding through the waves, and lower down, to the front of the ship, there are three triangular sails.

Apart from the crew, there are two hens, a goat and, next to their pens, three wooden buckets filled with earth, known as The Garden.

Once I had met everyone, the Captain told Harry to show me around. My cabin is on an upper deck and furnished plainly. However, my bed is a bunk against one wall, enclosed in a sort of three-sided box with a roof. It even has doors!

Captain Valentine sleeps in what I can only describe as a large wooden tea-tray, suspended from the ceiling. It looks extremely uncomfortable, all the swaying of a hammock but with none of the softness.

Lower down, the ship is dark and there is an overwhelming odour of mildew and ripe cheese. It is little wonder people are seasick. I felt queasy myself. The hold is packed with crates and barrels, some containing provisions for the voyage, others to be sold in New Paradise, with barely room to stand between them. The crew's quarters are as cramped. The men sleep on hammocks less than an arm's breadth apart.

June 13th

This morning I set about making myself more suitable clothes, turning my dress into breeches and my petticoats into tunic tops. As I worked up on deck, the wind constantly blew my ringlets into my eyes. My hair was no more suitable than my clothes I decided. It would have to be cut.

One of the crew who acts as ship's barber (and surgeon, should one of us be unfortunate enough to need a limb amputated) cropped my hair shorter than Harry's. Even the bearded giant looks at me with more approval now. I think he expected me to prove simply a nuisance. But truly free (for the first time) from the restrictions of Father, governesses and the conventions of home, I am determined to make the most of it!

While writing this entry, sea spray splashed my precious journal and I feared the ink would run. One of the sailors saw my concern and told me to wrap it in layers of oiled silk. It is what they keep the log books in. Nothing will protect it better, he promised. It will even survive a soaking if I drop it overboard. But I shall make sure that doesn't happen.

Thus, my second best pair of silk knickers (the ones Biddy insisted I carry with me at all times) have been torn into strips, thoroughly soaked in linseed oil and are presently drying in the watery sun.

June 24th

As one day merges into the next, my life as a 'landlubber' becomes a distant memory. I hardly have time to write this journal any more, there are so many chores to be done!

I share cooking and fire watching duties with Harry. I have even steered the ship (for one minute) under the bosun's watchful eye. I mend sails, polish the cannon and swab the deck until it shines.

There are only two things Captain Valentine has expressly forbidden me: to climb the masts or help with his navigation calculations. He said that no woman has a head for figures. Ha! But not even the second-in-command may interfere with his treasured compass and charts.

I did not think it prudent to tell Valentine that I have studied trigonometry and astronomy with my father since I was eight years old. But I do hope he knows what he is doing. From his frequent frowns and the comments of the crew, I have my doubts.

July 13th

Over the last few days, I have noticed a marked change in the climate. I am writing this up on deck, with a hot sun blazing down on my back, and warm breezes whipping the sails. Even the air seems different and the occasional cloud bursts are brief. The cold and smogs of home seem a very long way away. Perhaps we are nearing New Paradise at last.

July 15th

Today felt unsettled. I am writing this in my bunk, but for once it does not feel cosy and safe. There is a tension in the air, an uneasiness about the crew. I have a dreadful presentiment something awful is about to happen.

7

IN THE MIDDLE OF THE NIGHT

"Hello, darling!" Mrs. Curtis called cheerily, as she approached the cabin from the beach.

"Hi," Robyn muttered, without looking up. She hoped her mother wasn't about to give her a blow by blow account of the 'Eden experience'.

"Had a nice evening? It really is lovely here, isn't it? Oops!" said Mrs. Curtis, stumbling on the steps.

"Mmm," Robyn said, anxious to get back to Flora's adventure.

"What's that?" asked her mother, trying to see the cover of the typescript on Robyn's lap.

"*Moth-er*," Robyn protested. "I'm trying to read."

Mrs. Curtis giggled. "I would have thought you knew how by now!"

Despite herself, Robyn smiled at the ancient joke. Her mother had obviously had a good evening.

"What are you reading?" Mrs. Curtis asked again.

"It's a copy of a journal," Robyn answered. "Cautious Benjamin gave it to me – you know, the man from the museum. It was written two hundred years ago by the daughter of one of the governors here, but in those days this island was called New Paradise."

"Sounds fascinating," said her mother, "but don't stay up all night. I don't want you to be too tired to enjoy yourself. I'll see you in the morning." She gave Robyn a kiss. "Goodnight."

"'Night," said Robyn, heaving a sigh of relief and turning back to the journal.

July 17th

The day started badly when I spilt the hens' morning meal (ship's biscuits mashed with rum). Captain Valentine happened to be passing and berated me, saying that he wasn't running a ship for 'slip-shods and incompetents'.

Everyone seemed in low spirits, even Harry, and the goat was decidedly skittish. The bosun said a storm was on the way. With a wicked gleam in his eye he described wind and rain worse than a cat o' nine tails, that could lash the very clothes from your back.

As the day wore on, we grew more tense. Petty squabbles arose over the smallest things. Finally, Captain Valentine barricaded himself behind all the navigational equipment in his cabin and refused to come out.

He shouted in explanation that we were a long way from our destination, due to drifting caused by the wrong sort of wind, and he would be busy. The rest of us knew he had made a mistake in his calculations.

July 18th

Yesterday's supper was the last meal I ate with the crew. During the night the storm finally broke. The boat rocked so violently that the doors of my bunk were thrown open and I was flung onto the floor. Wind and rain swept through the ship, scattering all in their wake. Then there was the most terrifying crunch.

"She's hit rocks!" the bosun yelled in alarm. "She'll never survive this. The old girl isn't up to it!"

"ABANDON SHIP!" Valentine bellowed above the howling gale, (which sounded like beings in torment.)

Pausing only to snatch up this journal, I staggered up onto the deck, forcing my way against the wind. Two of the crew were struggling to untie the rowing boat and lower it over the side of the ship. The Pelican *had been speared by pointed rocks and was in its death throes. Every fresh wave and gust of wind tore into it, threatening to rip its very skeleton apart.*

The goat was slithering all over the deck. The first mate had tied a rope around her neck and was dragging her behind him as he tried to capture the terrified hens.

The bosun shouted for us all to get into the rowing boat, if we valued our lives. I could just make it out through the rain. In my opinion, the boat looked less likely to withstand the gale than The Pelican.

Feeling someone desperately pushing me from behind, I clambered over the rail and slid down a rope which hung over the ship into the rowing boat. Captain Valentine was on my tail, following so closely behind, I expected him to overtake me on the way down.

Once I was in the rowing boat, the others began to climb down. The first mate insisted on lowering the goat before he would get in himself, despite frantic pleas to hurry. If we were near The Pelican *when she went down, we would be sucked under with her.*

Suddenly, a mountainous wave crashed down upon us like an avalanche, lifting me out of the boat. I frantically kicked out, trying to catch hold of the boat but was caught up in the waves and whirled away.

"Man overboard!" someone roared.

I opened my mouth to scream for help and a gallon of salt water rushed in.

"For pity's sake help me!" I pleaded, coughing up sea. Through eyes blurred with seawater, I could just make out the boat, to my horror, being rowed in the opposite direction. Was that Valentine at the oars?

My strength was ebbing away, I felt exhausted and heavy, my clothes sodden. I was a deadweight being dragged down to the bottom of the ocean.

The next instant, something gripped my arm and shook me. From somewhere deep inside, I felt anger welling up, filling me with renewed strength. I would not give up so easily. I started to struggle.

"FLORA! DON'T!!" screamed a voice.

I feared I was delirious and thrashed my arms and legs in a final attempt to escape. I could not break free. It was too much. My shattered mind was hallucinating and I had no more strength to fight. My body went limp and the waves again washed over me.

I came to some while later, lying on a beach of the strangest black sand, the very beach I am writing on now, and coughing up water until my throat was raw. The voice had been no delusion, but Harry, who had dived in from the rowing boat to save me.

To my relief, my journal was almost completely dry! The oiled silk was a perfect protection. (It is not that I mind in the least about these jottings, but this journal is my last link with Father.)

We are on a beach not far from the wreck of The Pelican. *The ship, despite last night's gloomy predictions, is still largely in one piece and stuck on the rocks. No one had noticed how close we were to land in the fury of the storm. The rain masked everything. But if Captain Valentine had known our correct position, he would have realized we were near a safe harbour.*

If only he had rowed towards me instead of away. Who knows how or where he and the crew have ended up? I had grown quite fond of them, even Valentine. It is probably a forlorn wish, but I fervently hope they reached some safe shore.

Robyn yawned. *Some safe shore*, she read again. Unable to keep her eyes open any longer, Robyn picked up the copy of the journal and stumbled, yawning, to bed.

8

ON THE QUAY

Robyn was woken the next morning by the sun flooding into her room. Outside she could hear waves lapping the shore and in the distance, someone singing. A glorious day awaited her – more exploring and a chance to have a real look at the market.

She sprang out of bed and threw on a T-shirt and shorts. On the terrace, her mother was on her second cup of coffee. Robyn ate a chocolate muffin, gulped down a glass of orange juice and left, taking a slice of watermelon to eat on the bus into town.

She wandered through the chaos of the market, avoiding the mounds of ripe fruit which were piled on the ground, and smiling at everyone she passed. When she came to the museum, she turned left, walking along a sandy path which led her to the quayside.

To her surprise, there was Ben, sitting on a low wall,

watching a boat come in with its catch. The nets were full of little silver fish, sliding over each other, their scales flashing in the sun. Robyn stood hesitantly by the wall for a moment. Ben smiled as he recognized her.

"Hi!" he said, turning back to look at the sea.

"Hi!" she replied, feeling rather awkward. She looked into the distance and wished Melissa was there.

Suddenly, Ben's face lit up and he let out a huge shout. "ZACK!!" he yelled, almost deafening Robyn. "My brother," he explained.

A tall man in lime green shorts strode their way, jumped over the low wall and sat down. He had the same wide, lopsided smile as Ben.

Robyn was surprised. She hadn't expected Ben's brother to be so grown up.

"Robyn, this is Zack. Zack meet Robyn. Her mother's working for Gerry Sylvester," Ben said before Zack could say a word.

"Hi, Robyn," said Zack. "I've heard about your mother. She's doing Gerry's press campaign isn't she? I'm hoping to fix up a meeting with her, but Gerry seems to be keeping her to himself! He tells me she's got a very busy schedule."

"Mmm," said Robyn. How dull. All her mother ever seemed to do was have meetings.

Ben's voice broke into her thoughts. "Want to go out on a boat? Zack will take us, won't you Zack? Go on..."

"Not today, I'm afraid," Zack said firmly. "I've got an emergency IGPO meeting." Seeing the puzzled look on Robyn's face, he explained. "IGPO stands for the International Green Protection Organization. They keep an eye on the environment, check pollution levels at sea, monitor the welfare of wildlife in the area, and so on. I'm the Westward Islands' representative."

"Why the emergency meeting?" asked Ben.

Zack paused for a moment before he spoke. "There's something very wrong with the turtles. Here we are, almost at the end of the nesting season, and not even a quarter of them have laid any eggs."

Robyn listened with interest.

"These turtles only stop laying if they're unsettled, say, if something's disturbed them," Zack went on. "I've heard of it happening in other places, on islands crawling with tourists. You don't even need that many of them. Gerry and I were discussing it only yesterday. However 'caring' people are, the simple fact is, it doesn't take many visitors to drive animals away."

"But there's no one on Skull Island to disturb them," said Ben.

"I know," said Zack. "That's what I don't understand. I'm the only one who goes there – well, apart from the odd naturalist and I haven't seen any of those in the past year..." He shook his head.

Robyn and Ben didn't say anything. Zack's meeting was obviously very important. Even so, Robyn sighed, a boat trip would have been fun.

"Tell you what though," said Zack, breaking the silence. "Why not take *Francesca* out and go for a snorkel?"

"Who's Francesca?" asked Robyn.

Ben laughed. "*Francesca* is Zack's boat, idiot! His own boat, I mean, not the one he uses for work."

"Oh," said Robyn, reddening. "I didn't know."

"How could you?" Zack said kindly. "Don't tease!" he said to Ben, who grinned back, unabashed.

"I haven't got my swimming stuff with me," Robyn began, thinking that she ought really to check it out with her mother first.

"Well, I'd like Ben to do a couple of chores for me first," Zack said, looking hopefully at Ben. "Since I'm loaning you *Francesca*," he added.

"Doesn't sound as if I have much choice!" said Ben, with a grin.

"They shouldn't take more than an hour," Zack said. "Why don't you meet Robyn on the jetty in an hour and a half? It's near the Old Cotton Café, in Paradise Bay," he told Robyn.

"Meet you there!" cried Ben, chasing after Zack.

* * * * * * * * * *

Mrs. Curtis, working on maps for her brochure, was up to her eyes in cryptic symbols and signs. She looked up as Robyn entered. "Hello! You're back early."

"I've come for my swimsuit," Robyn said excitedly. "We're going out on a boat!" She paused. "If that's OK."

"Who's *we*?" asked her mother.

"Oh, me and Ben," Robyn explained. "You know, Mary's son, I met him yesterday. His brother's the warden of Skull Island!" she added.

51

"Mary?" her mother looked puzzled. "Oh, I know," her face cleared. "Mary the housekeeper. So Ben is Zack Joseph's brother. He's the IGPO rep. I've been hoping to meet him, but Gerry says he's almost impossible to get hold of as he's so busy."

"So can I go?" Robyn asked.

"Is Zack going too?"

"Um, no... but he's lending Ben his boat. It was Zack's idea."

"Well... OK then," her mother agreed at last. "But be careful." Robyn groaned and Mrs. Curtis smiled. "I know, I know. I'm a fussy mother and you're an excellent swimmer. But at least give your fussy mother some idea of when you'll be back."

"I'm not sure," said Robyn. "We'll probably only be a couple of hours." She went into the kitchen for a drink and Mrs. Curtis returned to her maps.

"Hey!" Robyn called suddenly. "Can I take some food? There's heaps in the fridge."

"Mmm," replied her mother absently, shading a shoreline. "Oh, Robyn," she added enthusiastically, "I had an idea about the brochure. Gerry's already produced a map of Paradise Island as it is today. I thought I'd add one showing what it was like a few hundred years ago. What do you think?"

"Yeah, great!" Robyn called. The fridge was so full it was hard to decide what to take... fresh pawpaw, tiny bananas, coconut cake, lime pie... Robyn laid a selection on the table, as her mother went on. "I've been reading up on the island's history. There were vast sugar plantations here, several mills, in fact the island was so prosperous there were even pirates..."

Robyn's ears pricked up. Pirates? But Mrs. Curtis was already caught up in her work again. Robyn drank some fruit juice and went to her room to put on her swimsuit under her shorts and T-shirt.

The copy of Flora's journal was lying neatly on her bedside table. Strange. She thought she'd left it on the floor by the bed. Then she noticed yesterday's clothes had been folded and placed on a chair.

Robyn wasn't used to anyone cleaning up after her. At home, her mother remained blissfully unaware of the state of her bedroom – unlike Melissa's mother, who constantly complained if the slightest thing was out of place. Melissa could use one of Eden's maids, Robyn thought.

She picked up the pages from the bedside table on her way out and reached the jetty well before Ben was due to arrive, which gave her plenty of time to carry on with Flora's adventure. Now, where was she? Last night she'd gone to bed just as Harry had rescued Flora during the storm...

9

A STRANGE COUNTRY

Several days after the great storm

As I write this, trees bloom around us and a cool breeze freshens the air. It is truly a remarkable place and today we plan to explore. But I am running ahead. I have to confess to not writing anything for several days. Now that I am finally having the adventure I longed for, writing is the last thing I think of. But I promised Father faithfully that I would record everything that happened to me, so here it is.

We are camped in a deserted cove. The beach stretches out in a perfect crescent, holding the jade and turquoise water in its sandy grasp. The whole place has an atmosphere of solitude about it. Harry and I might be the only humans here.

The previous entry I wrote several hours after Harry's valiant rescue. For a while after I came to my senses, we sat in silence, contemplating our situation. By great good fortune, we were only bruised, though between us, we had simply our tattered clothing and a small knife. By mid-afternoon, the sun was burning fiercely onto a surprisingly tranquil sea. Indeed, apart from the driftwood littering the beach, there was little to show for the storm the night before.

While I recovered, Harry made several trips to The Pelican, *salvaging an axe, Captain Valentine's telescope and pistol, (though no ammunition), and some soggy provisions. (At the time of writing, some days on, neither of us has had much luck in fishing yet. It seems rather tiresome to me, there's such an amount of waiting involved. However, there is an abundance of unusual and delicious fruits.)*

These last few days we have spent building a shelter. This took longer than it might have done, for we took plenty of breaks to swim and cool off. We constructed our hut out of branches and leaves. When wet, the sand becomes thick and sticky, almost like clay, and proves extremely useful for holding the branches and leaves together.

Harry shins up the steepest of trunks with ease, due, in no small part I am sure, to all his practice in the rigging. I take much longer. It is obviously what Father calls a 'knack'.

While Harry was up a most peculiar tree, with rings up its trunk, he hacked off a couple of large green fruits. (Peculiar at first sight, I should say. They are now more familiar. Indeed, the place is covered with these trees.) In any event, Harry lopped the top off one of the fruits with the axe (it took several attempts; the axe grows increasingly blunt). To our delight, it contained a watery liquid, not sweet, indeed almost sour, but most refreshing.

We have also explored a little of our surroundings. At the back of the beach, a sandy path winds its way up the side of a hill. Yesterday, we followed it as far as we could, passing a profusion of emerald green trees on our right. The path grew steeper and once or twice we paused to catch our breath, each time looking down to admire our (ramshackle) hut in its peaceful cove.

The air was hot and damp and I began to feel uncomfortable, even in my thin tunic. The path petered out by a group of trees and we went among them, hoping the shade would be cooler. Walking through the trees, we followed a river and reached a clearing.

Here, to our astonishment, the land rises up in a series of huge, rocky steps, like a giant's staircase. Water cascades down it in torrents, frothing as it goes.

Harry and I, struck with the same thought, looked at each other and smiled. As the thought came to me, I heard an echo of Biddy at her most horrified.

"Miss Flora! You wouldn't!"

Oh Biddy, I thought as I prepared to jump in, I would! The water was splendidly cool and for a while, Harry and I splashed each other and swam, or simply sat on a step feeling the water flood over us, until we had almost forgotten our predicament.

I have been writing this over a breakfast of pickled fish and mildewed cheese. Harry has just observed a thin line of smoke, curling up out of the trees and rocky hills some way ahead. It can only mean one thing: people! This place is inhabited, for all it feels so deserted in our cove. I must admit to being rather excited. Beautiful though this country undoubtedly is, I am anxious to go on, to New Paradise and Father. Where there are people, there will be boats and, surely, maps.

Harry, proving more cautious, fears they may not be friendly. Deciding that we may need to defend ourselves, he is presently chopping a stout stick. Not much of a weapon, I admit, but better than a pistol with no powder or shot. I shall chop one too; no doubt I can swing a stick as well as Harry. We plan to set off at once. I will attempt to chart our journey as we go.

[Photocopy of map attached – K. Phipps]

A map? thought Robyn. Where? She flicked through the typescript but there was no sign of a map. Disappointed, she found her place again and read on:

Midday

We have just discovered three such astounding things, that my hand is shaking as I write. Indeed, I hardly know with which find to begin.

Briefly, we headed inland, up the same sandy path we had taken before, this time walking beyond our glorious waterfall and on through the trees. After a while, they began to thin and we found ourselves atop the rocky hills we had glimpsed from the beach below.

From our vantage point, we realized we had landed

*on a fairly small island! There is a much larger
landmass to the north west, with clear signs of
habitation. We are confident that if we can build a
raft, from branches and possibly wood salvaged from*
The Pelican, *we should reach this landmass in a matter
of hours.*

*But to the second of our discoveries. The smoke
Harry espied is coming out of a mountain, which rises
above us. Evil-smelling fumes fill the air, worse than
the strongest smelling-salts you can imagine. Strangest
of all, the ground at the foot of this mountain gives off
its own heat.*

*Escaping the heat and stench, we walked quickly
on, and almost immediately came upon the third
incredible sight: a pool of thick, black sludge,
constantly churning, with occasional bubbles rising
up to burst on its surface.*

*As we stood there, transfixed, a terrible object rose
out of the pool: a leering, human skull. Harry and I
stared at it in amazed, excited horror. We watched,
mesmerised by its blank, staring eye sockets, until the
skull sank back beneath the sludge which closed over
it, as if it had never been.*

"Robyn!" called a voice. "Robyn!" But Robyn
hardly heard. She was with Flora and Harry by the
black, bubbling pool...

58

10

UNDERWATER

"Robyn!" the voice called a third time. Robyn put down the journal with a sigh, blinking as the black pool and volcano in her mind were replaced by bright fishing boats bobbing near the jetty.

"Robyn, didn't you hear me? I've been calling and calling." It was Ben, running red-faced up the sand. He waved a bag. "Ready to go?"

Robyn stood up, carefully tucking the copy of the journal into her backpack with the picnic.

"You bet!" she said, running onto the sand. "Where's Zack's boat?"

Ben pointed to a small blue and white craft, several boats along on the jetty. "I still can't believe it!" he said. "Zack lending us *Francesca*!"

"What's so amazing about that?" asked Robyn.

"It's a miracle," declared Ben. "She's his pride and

joy. He *never* lends her. His mind really must be on other things."

He held the boat steady as Robyn climbed in. Then he untied the mooring ropes, jumped in and started the motor, with the ease of someone who had been around boats all his life. They motored out into the bay and down the coast, past the Eden resort and its deserted beach, down to the tip of the island. They were almost at Skull Island, Robyn noticed excitedly.

"We'll stop on the coral reef," Ben said, as he cut the engine. Robyn looked at the shadowy dark mass, just below the surface, before gazing out to Skull Island, intrigued. It looked pretty ordinary, just a small island, covered in trees. But the stories around it made it seem different somehow, more exciting.

Ben moored the boat to a buoy, stripped to his trunks and pulled out an assortment of flippers and face masks from a locker at the back of the boat. "Ever used a snorkel before?" he asked.

"No," Robyn admitted, pulling her T-shirt over her head with a struggle. "But I'm a good swimmer. I mean, I've got my life-saving badge."

"Hope you don't need that!" said Ben. "Well, there's nothing to it," he assured her. "You've got the fins on your feet..." he picked up two huge, blue flippers, "...a face mask and the snorkel tube. That's it. Keep the tube above water and it's easy. If you want to dive, take a huge breath and hold it while you're underwater. When you surface, blow a huge breath out. That'll clear the tube."

"Right," said Robyn, doubtfully.

"And don't touch the coral," Ben added. "It's not a plant you see, it's a living creature. Well, hundreds of them actually. If you knock against them, they die. We try not to disturb anything. Knock the coral or upset the fish and Zack will be on the warpath!"

They put on the flippers and lowered themselves into the sea. Robyn waited while Ben put on his mask.

"Breathe in and make a good tight seal," he said, pausing before he pulled the mask over his eyes and nose. "Then breathe with your mouth through the snorkel tube. Oh, and one last thing. Don't kick your flippers too hard. You might frighten the fish!"

Robyn put on her mask, gripped the rubbery-tasting mouthpiece between her teeth, and checked to make sure the snorkel tube was upright. Ben gave her an encouraging thumbs-up sign and she ducked her head into the water.

At first, Robyn swam along the surface, holding her face underwater but keeping the snorkel tube well above the sea. But soon she grew more confident, gulping in a lungful of air to swim among the fish, before bursting back up into the open, blowing water out through the tube.

She was dazzled by the brightness – as if everything had been splashed with fluorescent paints. Schools of tiny, translucent fish darted by; red and white fish striped like candy chased black and white ones like mint humbugs. One had scales such a deep blue and gold, they looked like velvet.

But it was the coral which made Robyn really catch her breath – an underwater forest, with the weirdest plants and trees she'd ever seen. Coral like deer antlers; orange coral which was a mass of tentacles; white ridged coral spreading everywhere, like creeping brains. Fingers of coral reached up to the surface and sunlight. There were even clusters of fat yellow tubes, many taller than Robyn. "Sponges," Ben told her later.

Robyn spotted what seemed to be flowers growing out of a rock, but every time she went near, they snapped back out of sight.

On the third or fourth time she came up, to adjust her face mask, she happened to look back at Paradise and saw a tower poking through the tops of the trees. Robyn took off her face mask for a closer look. The area around it was overgrown, shrubs and bushes fighting for space.

"What's that?" she asked Ben when he surfaced.

He followed to where she was pointing. "That? It's an old sugar mill. But it's a ruin. The only way you can get to it is by sea. There's no road down to this part of the island."

"Can we take a look?" she said.

"Well..." said Ben, doubtfully.

"Have you ever been there?" asked Robyn.

"No," Ben admitted. "I don't think anyone has for a long time."

"All the more reason for us going," said Robyn excitedly. "Come on!"

11

EXPLORING

Quickly, they hauled themselves aboard *Francesca* and headed for the shore. Having pulled the boat well up onto the sand, they made their way through trees and up a grassy slope. It was a long climb up to the mill. This part of the island was totally still, and silent apart from occasional bird cries. Robyn almost felt she had to whisper.

"How long since anyone's been here, do you think?" she asked Ben quietly.

Ben shook his head. "No idea," he said. "It was abandoned after the great hurricane that wiped out all the sugar crops. But that was over seventy years ago. I doubt anyone goes near the place now..." He paused.

"Don't tell me," said Robyn. "It's cursed by the spirits of the dead mill owners!"

"You shouldn't make fun of things you don't

understand," Ben said, indignantly.

"Sorry," Robyn muttered. Couldn't he take a joke? She and Melissa were always teasing each other.

"This was once the richest estate on the island," Ben went on, sounding friendly again. "Sugar Point it was called. The owners were the wealthiest people on Paradise. But it wasn't a happy place, least, that's what my gran says. The first owner was a cruel man. In fact, he was the one who sent all those slaves over to Skull Island, and most of them never came back."

Robyn tried to imagine what this place had looked like then, but it was impossible to see it as anything other than overgrown jungle. Fighting her way through the bushes took almost all her concentration.

After a minute or two, they came to what looked like the remains of an old stone path. It had gone completely in some places and was very overgrown, but not impassable. Tangled creepers and thorny bushes ran wild, but they didn't seem to have covered the path with as much enthusiasm as the rest of the hill.

The path led to a series of rough stone steps which brought them up to the mill. Before them, a bridge spanned the river which once worked a water wheel. Beyond the bridge rose the grand, arched entrance to the mill, set in a cone-shaped tower. It was built out of a jumble of stones like a misshapen, three-dimensional mosaic.

"I think this tower might have been the chimney," said Ben, going under the arch. His voice echoed around the old curved stone walls.

"We might be the first people here since the mill was abandoned!" Robyn said, following him.

The chimney was open to the sky, encircling them like the turret of an ancient castle. They wandered around, looking up at the sky until they felt dizzy. Then they came out, going around the tower to explore a square stone building just behind it. The ground was littered with wood and rubble. Several doorways led off from one long, dark passage.

Robyn picked one at random and found herself inside an empty room, dark and dusty. The others were all the same. They wandered in and out of the old rooms for a while, making strange noises to hear how the echoes sounded. Ben was in the middle of one such call when his voice broke off abruptly. Silence. Robyn waited for a few seconds. "Ben?... Ben?" For a moment her heart thumped loudly. Then Ben appeared, a stunned expression on his face.

"Look at this," he said, leading her to a room at the back. There, in the supposedly deserted mill, were three battered chairs and an upside down packing case. Playing cards, empty drinks cans, apple cores and sandwich wrappers lay scattered over the floor.

"Someone *has* been here since the hurricane," Robyn murmured, "and recently..."

"It looks like people have been having a picnic here!" said Ben. "Who'd want to do that?" He wrinkled his nose in a frown. "Hey, I wonder if Gerry Sylvester knows about it? He wouldn't be impressed with all this litter."

At the mention of Gerry Sylvester, Robyn began to

wonder whether they should be there themselves. Perhaps this part of the island was out of bounds. It might even be the part Gerry planned to set aside for wildlife only.

"Maybe we'd better go," she said and they made their way back to the beach.

* * * * * * * * * *

It was almost dusk by the time they put Zack's boat away, still slightly puzzled by the mysterious visitors. Ben left Robyn at the bus stop, having arranged to meet her on Eden Beach the next day.

Back at the cabin, Robyn poured herself a mango milkshake, eager to continue Flora's journal. Taking her drink and a stack of cookies to the living room, she sank into the comfy sofa and took up where she had left off, by the black pool and its leering skull...

For a few seconds, I was speechless. As we stared into the pool, time seemed to stand still. Most peculiar of all: though the skull came out of thick, black sludge, not one drop stuck to it. (I know this seems impossible to believe.)

Father once showed me an experiment to prove that oil and water do not mix. I declare in all honesty, that the sludge rolled off that skull as if it was water running off oil, leaving it a deathly, bleached ivory white.

Once the skull had vanished, Harry and I looked at each other uncertainly for a moment. Had we really seen it, or were our minds playing tricks on us after the calamity of the storm and shipwreck?

"This is a most peculiar place," I observed. Harry nodded. With one last glance at the pool, we walked on. As we did, the island's unearthly silence struck me for the second time. Again, I was aware of how alone we were.

But such thoughts do not depress me for long. Determined to break the silence, I began telling Harry what I thought might await us in New Paradise. As the Governor's daughter, I foretold gloomily, I would have to attend balls and visit the sick. (Though I pray New Paradise proves less stuffy than home.)

I asked Harry why he had left his family to go to sea. But he doesn't have much of a family. His mother died when he was born; his father was hanged for stealing pears when Harry was four.

He and his older brother Jack grew up in an orphanage. Five years ago when Jack was fifteen, he was sent to New Paradise, one of a whole shipload of orphans, dispatched to be servants.

I was shocked. Orphans packaged up and sent off like boxes of tea! Harry swore to make his way out here to find Jack, and with no money to pay his passage, he sought work as a cabin boy. But no one wanted such a skinny, pale and weak-looking specimen as Harry, until he had a marvellous stroke of luck.

He was loitering by the docks, being shouted at by all and sundry, when he saw a man give a robust-looking lad a blow which sent him reeling. The lad ran off and the next thing Harry knew, someone in a bright red jacket appeared, furious because he now

67

had no cabin boy. Harry said that he had been at sea all his life and persuaded Captain Valentine (for it was he) to take him on.

By now we had left the rocky hills and were back among the trees. But the sun was setting and we wanted to be at our hut before nightfall. We decided to head back for 'supper', which, appetizing though it sounds, is, in fact, more mildewed cheese, though we also have ample selections of the sweetest, juiciest fruit.

Tomorrow, with our meagre possessions, we shall retrace our footsteps, continuing to the beach at the other end of the island, where we shall build our raft. On the journey back, we became rather lost among the trees, so Harry decided to climb one, the better to ascertain our position. He told me to climb up after him, should I be frightened by anything wild which might come along, though we have seen nothing but birds and fish so far.

"I have been to Bartholomew Fair!" I shouted to him, "There can be little more wild than that!" I smiled then, remembering the day I had escaped from Biddy. How long ago it seems now.

The following day

We have finished packing and are about to set off for the opposite end of the island.

Later

If only we had stayed where we were, and built the raft by our hut. We began well enough, following the path we took yesterday, past the waterfall and the black pool. But as we came out of the trees on the other side of the rocky hills, we were in for a surprise. A path led down to another cove, and there below, hidden from view until then, was a group of men!

They were sitting around a fire and swigging from bottles. We could hear raucous, drunken laughter and snatches of sea shanties. Anchored some way out was their ship, a tall, three-masted vessel floating on the tide. No need for a raft, I thought, with relief. Though I would have wished for friendlier-looking saviours.

I was ready to rush to our salvation, but Harry held back, saying we should be wary. We began to inch our way down the path, freezing whenever we moved too roughly, making for a boulder that would give us cover. We need not have been so timid. Whoever the men were, they were far too busy carousing to take the slightest notice of us. I doubt they would have heard a cannon going off.

Feeling quite confident, I stepped out from behind the boulder.

"Wait!" Harry whispered, pulling me back. He said he had a bad feeling and took Captain Valentine's telescope from his pocket. Putting the glass to his eye, he took a closer look at the ship beyond the bay.

What could he see? I asked him, noticing his drawn expression, excitement and fear mingling in my voice.

Harry's face was pinched and white as he turned to answer. They were flying the Jolly Roger, he told me, that fateful symbol of a bleached skull above crossed bones. For a moment, my heart stopped.

"Pirates!" I murmured in horror.

12

WHAT HAPPENED NEXT?

The copy of Flora's journal stopped there. Robyn was holding the last page of typescript. There was nothing more.

Is that it? Robyn thought disappointedly. Flora and Harry are face to face with pirates and I'll never know what happened next? A terrible thought struck her. What if the journal ended there because Flora had not been able to write any more? For a second, her mind filled with gruesome visions.

Robyn felt badly let-down. Cautious might have warned her that it didn't finish properly. She'd go and see him tomorrow. Maybe he knew what had happened to Flora and Harry. Just then, her mother broke into her thoughts.

"Hello, Robyn!" she cried, coming through the door from the veranda. "Did you have a good afternoon?

Mine was a disaster. The Minister for Tourism kept me waiting for an hour, then I was supposed to meet this brilliant marine engineer who's working with Gerry on some wonderful glass bottomed boat, but he'd already left by the time I arrived." She sank into a chair. "I know I shouldn't complain, these things do happen, but Gerry's been unavailable all day and Rick was really quite rude to me..."

"What a surprise," said Robyn.

"Come on," said Mrs. Curtis, sounding a little more cheerful. "Let's go for a walk on the beach and you can tell me all about your afternoon."

"You are enjoying yourself, aren't you?" she asked, as they strolled along Eden's beach in the moonlight. "I know it's rotten for you being on your own..."

"It's great... really," said Robyn, as a number of mosquitos homed in on her bare arms. "And I'm not on my own – there's Ben."

Mrs. Curtis waved a hand to disperse a small cloud of midges, but this only made them more determined. "Ow!" she said, as several latched onto her arm, seemingly attracted by the insect repellent rather than the reverse. "We'd better go in." She turned back to their cabin, then stopped. "No, I have a much better idea!" she said, winking at Robyn conspiratorially. "Let's escape Eden and visit the Angelfish Inn for supper."

Half an hour later, they were sitting at a table overlooking the sea, in front of large plates of flying fish and fries. "So how was the snorkel trip?" her mother asked. "Tell me from the beginning!"

71

Robyn swallowed. "Well, we took *Francesca,* Zack's boat, all the way down the coast and..."

"You know, Gerry's planning boat trips," Mrs. Curtis interrupted. "More like luxury mini-cruises, with an ecological theme. That's why I was supposed to be meeting him with the man who's designing the boats. But how am I meant to know what's going on if he keeps cutting appointments?" She broke off suddenly. "Oh I'm sorry Robyn, go on."

"There's a fantastic coral reef, just off the end of the island. The coral's weird but the fish are amazing. And then we..." She stopped. Should she mention the mill? They hadn't done any harm. Besides, there had been no big notices saying keep out.

"Then you?" Mrs. Curtis prompted.

"We looked around this old sugar mill," Robyn said casually. "It's right on the tip of Paradise, overlooking Skull Island. But there was a hurricane a long time ago and it's been abandoned ever since."

"This whole island has a fascinating history," said her mother. "In fact, there's a historical tour of the island tomorrow. I thought we might enjoy that."

"*We*?" said Robyn.

"It'll be fun," her mother smiled. "Something we can do together. It's tomorrow morning."

"I said I'd see Ben tomorrow," Robyn began.

"It's organized by one of the locals who's a bit of a history buff," Mrs. Curtis continued, as if Robyn hadn't spoken. "It's the man who runs the museum."

"Cautious Benjamin," said Robyn, suddenly remembering the unfinished journal. She frowned.

"Are you OK?" asked her mother. "Don't you like your fish?"

"It's just the journal..." She saw her mother's puzzled expression and explained. "Remember I was telling you about the girl in the painting, the one in the Governor's Mansion?"

"Mmm?" said Mrs. Curtis, who clearly didn't.

"Well, the girl is Flora and she was the Governor's daughter and she was coming to meet him when she was shipwrecked. He'd given her a notebook before he left and she kept a journal in it and Cautious lent me a typed copy because the original's in his museum and I've just reached an exciting part and there's no more." Robyn came to a halt, a little red in the face.

"Is that Flora as in Flora and Harry?" said her mother.

"Yes!" cried Robyn, astounded. "How do you know?"

Mrs. Curtis coughed. "I came in last night to say goodnight and you were asleep. I saw the typed pages on the floor, wondered what they were and glanced through them. I was absolutely engrossed. I borrowed them to read in bed but I *thought* I'd put them all back. I only read the beginning, but it was fascinating. I think there's an interesting angle on this for my publicity campaign, a slice of 'real history'!"

"Oh!" Robyn groaned so loudly that the other diners looked up in astonishment. "You might have told me. I was really enjoying it."

"Dessert?" said a waiter, arriving at that moment to clear their plates away.

"Yes please!" said Mrs. Curtis.

But Robyn had already pushed back her chair. "I'm full to the brim," she said. "I don't think I could eat another thing."

"You must have room for some ice cream," said her mother. "Besides, it's so nice to sit and chat like this. We never have the chance at home."

So Robyn had no choice but to sit and eat a huge double chocolate and passion fruit sundae while telling her mother more about Ben. The ice cream was good, but she was itching to get back to the journal.

Soon the waiter was back again. "Coffee?" he asked.

Robyn looked at her mother, not saying anything, but silently willing her, 'Please can we go now, *pleeease.*'

Mrs. Curtis smiled. "Just the bill thank you!"

At last! thought Robyn exultantly. She tapped her feet impatiently on the floor, wondering if she could go on ahead.

"No charge, of course, Mrs. Curtis," smiled the waiter. "Compliments of Gerry Sylvester."

Robyn raced along the beach to the cabin. What had happened to Flora and Harry after they had come across the pirates?

13

NO ESCAPE!

There were several more pages, half-hidden under her mother's bed. Robyn eagerly picked them up and took them to the sofa. Stretching out, she began to read.

NB: entries in subsequent pages are erratic, with text wandering all over the page. They are also difficult to decipher, owing to the conditions under which they were written – K.P.

What conditions? thought Robyn, intrigued.

The following is so vivid, it might have happened minutes ago. We immediately resolved to return to our hut with all speed. Thanks to Harry, the men had not seen us. With luck they would not venture to our end of the island. Once we had built our raft, we would set sail from there.

While half of me lauded this plan as sensible, yet the other half was disappointed. Pirates! After the shipwreck, this was the most exciting (albeit frightening) thing that had ever happened to me. Pirates were something you only heard about, but here we were almost face to face with them! I wanted to wait a while and watch some more.

Reluctantly, I followed Harry, turning back for one last glimpse. It was to prove my downfall. I missed my footing and slid down the hillside.

I desperately tried to catch hold of something as I fell, but grasped only clumps of damp ferns which slipped through my hands. I fell a few hundred yards and lay there, shaken and gasping for breath. That was the least of my worries. My fall had alerted the men on the beach below.

A pirate in a dark shirt jumped unsteadily to his feet, drunkenly waving a cutlass. He was shouting but the words were slurred and indistinct. Suddenly, all the men were standing up and shouting. A tall man, with a long nose and pointed beard, who had been sitting apart from the others, whipped out a pistol and fired into the air. As I saw him, I heard a distant voice. 'Beware of the man with the pointed black beard...'

"SILENZ!" the man bellowed. A shocked hush descended. He pointed the pistol at me and waved me to come down. Harry came out from behind the boulder and joined me. His face was closed.

"DOWN!" we were ordered and grimly, we obeyed.

The man who had fired the pistol snapped out a command. One of the men tied our hands behind our backs. Then we were pushed roughly onto the sand, made to sit with our backs against each other and bound with more rope. It cut into my arms and the knot dug into my side, but I did not dare cry out.

The leader began to fire questions at us, as fiercely as he had fired the weapon a minute earlier. I shall remember every word as long as I live.

"You dared come here, despite all the tales? No one sets foot on this island. Did you not see the ring of skulls? Or perhaps the spirits hold no fears for you? Are you foolhardy or just plain foolish? Answer me!"

I had no idea what he was talking about. "We... we were shipwrecked," I stammered incoherently. I felt a sour sickness rise up inside me, burning the back of my throat.

The man drew a long-bladed knife from his belt, running a dirty finger along it to show us how sharp it was. Harry seemed mesmerised by the knife, winking in the light.

"Such a pity you were washed up here," the man sneered. He glanced at a stack of barrels and frowned. "But why should I believe this shipwreck story? I see no ship, no crew. Were you the only ones to survive?"

Suddenly his knife was at Harry's throat. "Tell me the truth," he whispered threateningly through clenched teeth. "TELL ME THE TRUTH!"

"We are," I cried, almost sobbing. My heart was thumping so heavily in my chest, I felt it would surely explode. My eyes filled with hot tears which I angrily blinked away.

"We were on The Pelican *under Captain Valentine when it struck a rock during a storm. The others escaped by rowing boat,*" Harry said dully, as if cowed into submission.

The man grinned, curving his lips around stained teeth. His eyes glittered, hard and mean. He began to speak rapidly, a torrent of words spewing from his mouth, almost too fast to hear. He talked of skulls and souls and spirits. I was certain he meant to kill us. The waiting was agony but the end looked a thousand-fold worse.

He paced back and forth in front of us, revelling in our helplessness. Once he spat onto the sand and laughed. The other pirates watched his every move.

But all the while he was speaking, Harry was working steadily at the bonds which tied our hands. The pirates had been too drunk to knot them properly. At length, our hands were free. I slowly eased my hand around to the knot at my waist. Soon the rope which held us together was undone also.

But how could we escape? What match were we for half a dozen men, at least one of whom had a pistol? We were trapped. I could see no way out.

14

WHERE'S ZACK?

That was the last page. Robyn flicked through the other pages, hoping some had been misplaced. They hadn't. She began to rock on her cane chair until it creaked alarmingly.

Mrs. Curtis looked up from the table and an array of maps. "Robyn, I'm trying to work," she said, sounding distracted and slightly irritated.

"There are still some pages missing from the journal," Robyn complained.

"I thought you took the last few from my bedroom. Did you leave any behind?"

But there were no more pages in the bedroom. Robyn came back into the living room, stood over her mother and sighed heavily.

"I can't find any, only it breaks off in the middle of her story, you see, and..."

"Robyn, I'm sorry... I'm trying to work," Mrs. Curtis repeated. She sighed. "I have to get this finished tonight. Why don't you go to bed? You're sounding grumpy and that always happens when you're overtired." She looked up and blew Robyn a kiss. "'Night. Sleep well."

* * * * * * * * * *

Mrs. Curtis was up bright and early the following morning. Robyn heard her singing in the bathroom, as she lay in bed after a restless night, dreaming of pirates.

"Robyn, come and have breakfast!" her mother called. "The minibus is leaving at nine thirty. There are several other guests going on the history tour. We mustn't keep them waiting."

On the terrace, Robyn ate a pineapple yoghurt and listened to her mother chat about 'Historical Cruises', a brainwave she had had during the night.

"Thinking about the tour?" her mother asked.

"Mmm," said Robyn, who was thinking of the other guests and wishing she could have been off somewhere exploring with Ben.

The Eden driver dropped them off at the Old Cotton Café, by a makeshift sign which proclaimed:

PARADISE AND THE PAST
A walking tour conducted by C. Benjamin
WAIT HERE
Leaves around 10:00 on Thursdays

Only a few minutes later, Cautious Benjamin arrived. "Hello again," he beamed to Robyn. "You here for my tour?" He nodded to Mrs. Curtis, who smiled and gave him a firm handshake.

"Julia Curtis," she said. "P.R. Consultant for Gerry Sylvester. How do you do, Mr. Cautious!"

"Delighted!" he replied. "By the way, Robyn," he added, "I came across some more pages of that typescript of Flora's journal this morning." He waved some blue and green papers at her. "I was looking for these tour maps, and there they were. Funny, I don't know how those pages came to be separated from the rest." Cautious shrugged. "Anyhow, I put them on the shelf by the door. Pick 'em up any time – museum's always open."

"I could go now," said Robyn eagerly.

"But darling, you don't want to miss the tour," said her mother.

Cautious cleared his throat. "Hello everyone and welcome! Follow me back through the mists of time. First stop, Paradise Beach, named after the explorer Juan Paradiso who landed there in June 1547. You might say he was the island's first European tourist!"

They walked through the market, past wooden houses with peeling pink and yellow paint, onto a wide beach. They grouped around the jetty as Cautious stared out to sea.

"Well then, here we are," he said, turning to the group. "This is the very spot where Juan Paradiso landed all that time ago – sea sick no doubt, he wasn't a very good sailor by all accounts. He set up a small settlement here, left some of his crew and then hot-footed it back to Europe, laden with exotic fruits and spices."

"Did he ever return?" asked someone.

"Yup, six years on, only to find his settlement wiped out by plague and the British ruling the roost. Poor man was furious! Died of swamp fever just two weeks later. Anyhow, the British got the sugar plantations up and running and that's when the pirates appeared!"

Pirates? thought Robyn. Just then she thought she heard someone call her.

"Robyn!" It was Ben. He'd appeared from nowhere and was grabbing her arm.

"What is it?" she cried, remembering with a guilty jolt that she had agreed to meet him on Eden Beach. But Ben seemed to have forgotten too.

"It's Zack," he said. "There's a problem. Can you come?" The look on Ben's face told Robyn that he was deadly serious.

As he spoke, Cautious looked up and noticed them. "You two young 'uns want to explore on your own?" he called.

Ben nodded vehemently.

"Is that OK?" said Robyn, turning to her mother.

Mrs. Curtis was busily scribbling in her notebook. "All right," she muttered, without looking up. "If you must."

"See you later, then," said Robyn. She turned to Ben. "What is it?"

"It's Zack. He went out first thing to Skull Island, before dawn... it was still dark. He's worried about something, but he wouldn't tell me what. Anyway, he said it wouldn't take more than an hour or two, but that was more than five hours ago. Besides, he had to be back in time for an IGPO meeting this morning. That's why he left so early..."

"So what do you want to do?" asked Robyn.

"Umm, I think..." He paused. "I think we should go to Skull Island to look for him," he said miserably. "I know we're not supposed to go over there," Ben sounded reluctant, "but it's the only place he can be. I've looked everywhere else."

"*Skull Island*!" murmured Robyn, feeling a tingling down her spine. "Do you really think we should? I suppose if Zack's in trouble it might be OK..." The prospect of visiting the forbidden island with its strange, magical history was terrifying yet thrilling all at the same time.

"I think this is an emergency," Ben said, as if trying to persuade himself.

"Come on then!" said Robyn.

Leaving Mrs. Curtis and the others laughing at one of Cautious's jokes, they ran to the jetty.

"We'll take *Francesca*," Ben said, quickly untying the mooring ropes. "Zack will have gone over in the boat he uses for work. It's newer and faster."

Soon Ben was steering a course down the length of Paradise Island, biting his bottom lip nervously. "Skull Island's tricky to navigate, because of the reef," he said. "There's only one safe approach. We'll have to land on the beach on the far side of the island."

Robyn watched Skull Island loom closer. Home of

spirits, she thought excitedly – though the image in her head, of skulls on spikes, was creepy. *Francesca* slipped silently through the water. They rounded the reef and came ashore in a deserted, crescent-shaped cove. But as the boat bumped onto the sand, Ben's hesitation returned. He seemed to have lost his sense of urgency, sitting stiff as a statue.

The island was still, and silent, save for the gentle splashing of the waves. A bird's plaintive cry broke the silence, making Robyn jump. For some reason she shivered, though the air felt much hotter here than on Paradise.

The island seemed to have a brooding presence. It had seen some terrible things. Robyn remembered the hundreds of slaves who had met their deaths here and shivered again. Even with Ben beside her, she felt inexplicably lonely. There was no sign of Zack's launch. They climbed out of the boat and began to walk up the beach.

"Where should we go first?" Robyn was asking, when Ben gasped. She looked up to see his face turn white.

"Zack?" he croaked. He sounded petrified. Robyn followed to where his finger was pointing. There on the beach in front of them was a set of footprints. Footprints which went up to a sandy path and stopped beside a rock, on which there lay a torn shirt soaked in blood.

15

WHO'S THERE?

Ben and Robyn stared at it in horror. "Zack..." Ben said again, in a hollow voice.

Robyn knelt down for a closer look. "Is this Zack's shirt?"

Ben shrugged.

"Maybe he just cut himself on something..." Robyn's voice died away. It sounded lame, even to her. "Well, we have to find him," she added, sounding more positive than she felt. "And the sooner the better."

A trail of blood spots led away from the rock along the sandy path. Hearts thumping, they followed it, winding their way steeply up the side of a hill, passing a mass of trees on their right. Once or twice they paused to catch their breath, looking down on the cove. The path pctered out on the edge of a forest. Climbing up, Robyn had felt fine. Now, among the trees, she felt as

85

if dozens of unseen eyes were watching her.

Something rustled. She jumped. What was that? It was only a parrot flying out of the trees. They went deeper. Little sunlight could force its way between the trees here. Strange shadows fell across their path. The jungle was oppressively warm, yet Robyn felt cold.

"This is hopeless," said Ben, ten minutes later. "We're just going around in circles."

As he spoke, Robyn caught a flash of white clothing some way ahead. "Look, over there!"

"At last!" Ben cried, but his relief turned to disappointment. "No," he said, "That's not Zack."

A man was sitting against a tree, talking into a mini-tape recorder. He wore a white T-shirt, and had a piece of torn, bloodstained material bound around his left arm. He didn't notice them.

"Who is he? What's he doing here?" Robyn mouthed to Ben, who shrugged.

"And where's Zack?" he mouthed in reply.

They hid behind a tree and watched the man for a few moments, straining to hear what he said. "...valuable hardwood, redwood, ebony..."

Ben nudged Robyn uneasily and pointed back the way they had come. Something told him that it wasn't a good idea for the man to spot them. "Better leave before he sees us," Ben mouthed.

But the man had finished whatever it was he was doing. He stood up, nursing his arm. Robyn and Ben left as quietly as they could. Robyn went to follow Ben and her T-shirt snagged on a bush. As she tried to free herself, urgently pulling away, the bush shook.

The man was instantly alert. "Who's there?"

"Remember, he has no more right to be here than us," Ben whispered to Robyn, before coming out from behind the tree.

The man approached, giving Ben a chance to see his face clearly.

"Mr. Lucas!" he cried in surprise.

"Rick?!" exclaimed Robyn. It was Mr. Sunglasses minus his sunglasses. He looked very different without them.

A range of expressions chased across Rick's face. For a second, he looked horrified. Then his face hardened, before breaking unexpectedly into a smile.

"Hi!" he said, and groaned. "Sorry, as you can see I've, aagh, gashed my arm. I was just carrying out a little private research for a... a little project of mine."

It was true, Robyn remembered, you could apply for a visitor's research permit. But Ben wanted to know more. "Why are you here, exactly?" he demanded.

"Checking on the turtles!" Rick said smoothly. "They're something of a hobby."

"Does my brother know you're here?" Ben asked, at the same time as Robyn fired a question of her own.

"If you're checking on the turtles, what are you doing in the *forest*?"

"Aagh! I'm sorry, what was that? My arm's so painful, it's hard to concentrate. But tell me," he said, wincing, "What are *you* doing here?"

"We're doing something for my brother," Ben said briefly. He sounded more confident than she felt, Robyn thought, her heart racing.

"Zack's *here*?" said Rick, his smile faltering for a moment. His face paled. Seeing his cheeks whiten, Robyn looked at Rick's arm. The bloodstain on his makeshift bandage was spreading.

"That looks bad," she said. "How did you do it?"

Rick glanced down. "I, er, tripped and gashed it on a rock. I'm sure I'll be fine." He stood up slowly, swaying on his feet. "Oh!" he said. "It's all gone dark!" Robyn and Ben rushed to support him. "Thanks!" he said. "I thought I was going to faint! I don't know, a little cut and... well, not so little actually."

He paused, leaning back against a tree for support. "Could you do something for me?"

"What?" said Ben suspiciously.

"I don't think I can steer my boat in this state. I don't suppose you would take me back to Paradise?"

Ben's face was hard. "We're doing something really important," he said.

"Look at him," Robyn said quietly. Rick moaned.

"I suppose we'll have to," said Ben.

"Thanks, you don't know how grateful..." Rick began.

"Where is your boat?" Ben broke in bluntly. "We didn't see it."

"Um, on the other side of the island," Rick said quickly. "Don't worry, it can stay there for now. I really should get back. I'll probably need a tetanus shot."

Once on *Francesca*, Rick slumped in the prow. Ben headed back to Paradise at top speed. At the jetty, Rick stood up.

"Thank you. I really am grateful. I'm sure I'll be

all right from here." He climbed ashore with surprising agility for someone who had been leaning on trees minutes earlier.

"Perhaps we'd better come with you," said Ben, leaping out of the boat. Robyn followed.

"No really, I'll manage," Rick insisted. He smiled. "But thanks again. Oh, one more thing. Please don't mention this to your brother. I feel a bit of a fool... and I hate to think what Gerry would say."

Robyn and Ben watched him walking up the beach holding his arm. After a moment, Robyn drew her eyebrows together in a frown.

"What's up?" Ben said, turning to Robyn. She was standing immobile, staring after Rick. "Robyn?"

"Huh?" she said. "Sorry, I was just thinking... it's odd, isn't it?"

"What is?" Ben asked, nonplussed.

"Rick... I mean, he was very talkative, almost friendly. And he felt better very quickly, didn't he? Once we got here, I mean."

"Um," said Ben. "He was probably just relieved to be back on Paradise."

"He didn't answer my question either," Robyn added. "Why was he checking up on the turtles in the forest? And did he really cut his arm on a rock?"

But Ben was still worried about Zack. What if Rick's cut had something to do with Zack's disappearance? What if they'd had a fight?

"Never mind about Lucas," Ben said grimly. "We must find Zack."

16

THE END

Before Ben had a chance to say more, the noise of a powerful outboard motor broke their thoughtful, worried silence.

Ben grinned with relief. "Zack!" he cried. "ZACK!" he repeated, indignantly this time, as Zack pulled up alongside the jetty in his IGPO boat. "Where were you? What happened?"

"Don't ask," Zack said. "It's been one of those mornings. While I was on Skull Island I had a radio message to visit one of the smaller islands to the north of Paradise, and just as I was leaving there, I picked up a distress signal from a yacht in trouble, which took a long time to sort out. I am sorry."

"Oh," said Ben. "Only you *did* say the IGPO meeting was important."

"I know," Zack said ruefully, neatly throwing a rope

over the mooring post and swiftly securing it. "I radioed ahead and they agreed to postpone the meeting till this evening. Were you worried?"

Robyn waited to hear Ben's reply.

"Oh, we were all set to send out a search party!" Ben said casually. "You came back just in time."

Perhaps Zack would be angry if he'd known they'd actually gone onto Skull Island, Robyn thought, watching them. They shared the same easy banter as Melissa and her two younger brothers.

"How about some ice cream to celebrate my safe return," Zack suggested. "Coming, Robyn?"

"Oh, no thanks," she said, feeling like an outsider. "I have to get something from the museum. See you later."

"See you," said Ben, following Zack, jogging to keep up with his lengthy strides.

Robyn left the jetty and headed straight for the museum, eager to read the last pages of the journal. It took a while, but she enjoyed the walk and the sights, sounds and smells of the market which were almost familiar to her now.

She arrived at the old fort and went inside. It was empty and completely quiet, as if waiting for visitors before it would come to life. Where had Cautious said he'd left the pages? She looked around. On a shelf by the door... got it! Robyn climbed up on a chair to retrieve them and went back outside.

She had planned to take them back to the cabin and raid the fridge before reading on, but with the journal actually in her hands, she knew she couldn't wait another minute. Sitting down under a red-flowering tree by the museum, she lost herself in the adventure. Harry had untied them, but he and Flora were still surrounded by brutish pirates...

Suddenly, Harry grasped my arm. "Now!" he whispered, "Go!" I leapt to my feet and followed him as he ran past our astonished captors. The element of surprise gave us a great advantage and I felt a sense of relief, no, exhilaration, as we ran. Perhaps we might escape. My joy was short-lived.

The pirates shook themselves out of their drunken stupor and chased us. I despaired. With the sea ahead and pirates behind, we were trapped. Harry ran to the right, urging me to follow. I was bewildered. He was heading straight for a cliff. Then at the last moment, I spotted it: a gap between two rocks in the cliff face. Harry dived through it, dragging me with him into a cave.

I heard the man with the gun speak for the last time. "If they have discovered our tunnel, they must be killed on the spot."

My blood ran cold at his words, for there ahead of us was indeed a tunnel! We ran down it until the roof grew lower. Then we scrambled along, our backs stooped and our heads bent low.

Several pirates chased us. We could hear their grunts echoing behind. Then the tunnel forked in two. Harry chose the left fork. Being by far the narrower of the two, he said, would hinder the men in their attempts to follow us. We found ourselves in another, even smaller cave which led into a vast one. Indeed, tunnels led off in every direction!

To our great relief, so far the pirates have not followed. Nor have we heard their shouts for some time. I cannot be certain but hope with all my heart that they have gone. We assume they are waiting for us to come out again. I suppose we now have to wait for them to give up.

By a great stroke of luck, we have some food with us, having been prepared to stay out all day. However, this has been rationed and with my hunger pangs barely assuaged, I am now extremely thirsty.

Several hours later

It is to be hoped that the pirates are an impatient bunch and have already given up on us. We seem to have been in this cave so long.

I have been writing this by candlelight, one of several candles Harry had by chance in his pocket. He has left me scribbling, while he investigates other tunnels. He feels hopeful that there may be an alternative way out.

In the candle's flickering light, I can see a series of crude carvings upon the walls. They are pictures of skulls, hideous skulls, all of varying sizes, but all with the same menacing leer. What dreadful place is this?

Some hours later still

Harry has come back several times, to report no success as yet, though he keeps stumbling across heaps of old and crumbling bones. Is this some terrible

*omen? I fear we will never escape. My only comfort is
that the pirates have not reached us. I shudder to think
how we might have died at their merciless hands. The
last candle has burned almost to nothing. The flame
gutters. Soon there will be only a pool of wax left.*

*If anyone should ever find this journal, please tell
my Father how truly sorry I am. I did not mean to
cause such distress. To lose me as well as Mother...*

*How could I have foreseen things turning out thus?
Will my Father ever read this? Will anyone?*

*If it should reach you, Father, I love you. Be strong.
Harry is calling. The light grows dim.*

It stopped there. At the bottom of the last page
someone had scribbled four words in pencil. 'The
journal ends here.' Robyn was too wrapped up in
Flora's last words to wonder why this note was
handwritten. All the other notes had been typed and
initialled by KP – Ken Phipps, the man who had
worked on the typescript.

What had happened to Flora and Harry, Robyn
wondered. Did they escape the pirates? Did they find
a way out of the caves? Did they ever reach New
Paradise? Now she would never know. For this really
was the end of the journal.

She stood up to stretch her legs. She felt stiff, and
very hungry, so she wandered back to the market to
wait for a bus. Ben was sitting at the bus stop.

"Hey!" he said. "I thought you'd be in your cabin.
I was just coming to see you."

"Oh?" said Robyn. "I've just been reading a copy

of this two-hundred-year old journal in the museum," she explained. "It's about this amazing girl called Flora and a cabin boy, Harry, and they..."

But Ben wasn't listening. "Look, I told Zack about Rick Lucas. I had to. We couldn't keep it to ourselves. He might have been up to anything. What if he harms the turtles, even if only by accident? What would we tell Zack then?"

"No, you're right, you had to tell him," said Robyn. "What did he say?"

"He was mad at us for going over at first, even though he knew how worried I'd been. But when I told him about Lucas, he quickly changed his tune."

"Why?" Robyn asked.

"Because Lucas has never applied for a research permit. Zack said Lucas wouldn't know a turtle if one bit him on the toe! He thinks Lucas is up to something, but he wouldn't say what. Anyway, Zack's really worried. He's going back to Skull Island tonight, after his meeting, and he wants us to go too. We can show him where we found the blood-stained shirt and where we came across Lucas."

"Great," said Robyn, with an exhilarating mixture of fear and excitement. They were going back to Skull Island at night! "I'll have to check with my mother first, though," she added.

"OK," Ben said. "We'll call for you about eight. Zack's determined to find out what's going on."

17

A SHOCKING DISCOVERY

Back at the cabin, after a huge lunch, Robyn began another postcard.

Dear Mel,
I've been to this amazing island! It's called skull Island and it's haunted by spirits (so they say). We didn't see any though - or any skulls, even though the island's supposed to be littered with them. But we're going back tonight (!) so it might be spookier. 'We' is me and Ben, who's this boy I met here, and his brother, who's warden of skull Island. Their mother works for Gerry.

Robyn put down her pen. Though she was writing to Melissa, she couldn't stop thinking about Flora. The excitement of returning to Skull Island added to her general feeling of restlessness, so she decided to go for a swim. For once, there were only a few people around the pool, chatting over drinks. The serious swimmer in goggles was nowhere to be seen, so Robyn had fun, splashing around and floating on her back, gazing up at the sky. When she came out, she flopped on one of the sunloungers to dry in the sun. The warm, still air seemed to cushion her. There was hardly a sound. Eden was as peaceful as ever. As the sun slowly sank into the sea, Robyn fell into a doze...

...She was stepping into a boat which rocked her gently. Then mounds of fruit appeared on the floor at her feet. Fresh juicy pineapples, and melons with shining rinds and delicate scents. But they rotted before her eyes, maggoty, mildewed, pungent. The maggots were everywhere, devouring the fruit, squirming on the floor at her feet. They were almost upon her when they vanished. In their place sat a deathly, bleached ivory skull.

Suddenly, the boat went too and she was deep underground, in an enormous cave, full of holes like a Swiss cheese. It was pitch black inside... until a strange, green fluorescent light crept into the corners. The light shone through the holes illuminating them. All at once, Robyn saw rows of skulls, leering at her, grinning between chipped, brown teeth. Everywhere she looked she could see them. Row upon row of menacing skulls. And now she could hear footsteps, running...

"Grab her!" a voice shouted.

The footsteps came closer, Robyn desperately looked for a way out but every hole was blocked by a skull. Right in front of her, the monstrous mouth of one of the skulls began to yawn, a gaping chasm so wide Robyn thought its jaw would drop off. But it kept widening and the skull seemed to grow with it. Robyn shivered. The footsteps sounded so close now, her pursuers must be almost upon her.

Taking a deep breath she took the only exit she could see – into the cavernous mouth of the skull. Its jaw snapped shut and Robyn was trapped, left in darkness but at least alone. Then a disembodied voice began to call her name...

"Robyn? Robyn? Can you hear me Robyn...?"

Robyn curled up into a ball, her hands over her head, sinking deeper and deeper into the void.

"Robyn!"

"Leave me alone," she whimpered. "Whoever you are, leave me alone..." To her horror, something began to shake her.

"Robyn, are you OK? What's the matter?" asked someone in a worried voice. Robyn opened her eyes to see her mother standing over her.

"At last!" Mrs. Curtis said, as Robyn blinked in confusion. "Listen darling, Gerry's organized an evening of traditional music and dance at the Old Cotton Café. He's been raving about the amazing local talent. He says everyone on the island can play an instrument! Come with me. It'll be great fun!"

"But I sort of promised Ben I'd do something with him. Zack's taking us on a night-time boat trip!" Robyn said, looking at her mother hopefully.

"A *night*-time boat trip?" said Mrs. Curtis. "Oh." She sounded disappointed. "Are you *sure* you don't want to come with me?"

Robyn was.

"Well, tell me more," said her mother, relenting slightly. "Where are you going and how long for?"

"Just around the island," Robyn said. She didn't need to tell her mother which one. "We won't be more than a couple of hours."

"Hmm..." said her mother. Robyn waited. "And you say Zack's taking you?" Robyn nodded. "You know, I finally managed to meet him this afternoon," Mrs. Curtis continued. "No thanks to Rick Lucas who hadn't passed on any of my messages to him. I was impressed by Zack Joseph. Very committed. Passionate about wildlife."

"Oh he is!" said Robyn. "And very responsible." Commitment and responsibility mattered a lot to her mother. Robyn looked up at her, silently pleading.

"Yes, OK, you can go," Mrs. Curtis said finally. "But be sure to do what Zack tells you."

They walked back to the cabin together, where Mrs. Curtis briefly touched up her lipstick. "I'm going now, Robyn. Have a good time!" she called as she left.

* * * * * * * * * *

It was getting late and Robyn was on her fifth trip to the fridge for a snack, when there was a knock at the door.

"All set?" said Ben. "Sorry we're so late. Zack's meeting went on and on. He's waiting for us in the IGPO boat."

"Hi, Robyn," Zack said in a low voice, as she rolled up her jeans and waded out to the boat that lay just off the shore of Eden Beach. "Jump aboard." He started the engine without another word and they sped off.

Paradise looked beautiful at night. The lights from Gerry's Bar lit up the sky and cast faint reflections on the water. The sea was almost as bright as the sky, rippling with the reflections of neon fish.

Before long, Skull Island loomed ahead. Zack motored into the cove they had landed on earlier in the day. They headed to the beach and pulled the boat ashore.

"Where was Rick Lucas when you first saw him?" Zack asked.

"In the forest," Ben ran ahead, "But the footprints were here." He pointed to the path.

"And the bloody shirt's here," said Robyn, going up to the rock. "Oh," she cried. It was gone.

"Hmm," said Zack.

"We're not making it up," Ben insisted.

"No, no, of course not," Zack murmured. "And you didn't see Rick's boat?" he confirmed.

"No, he told us he'd left it on the other side of the island," Ben said.

"Really?" said Zack. "How on earth did he... Hold on, what was that?"

"What was what?" asked Ben nervously.

"I think I heard something," his brother said. "I'm just going to check." He took out a flashlight. "Will you both wait here for me? I won't be long – maybe five minutes. Then you can show me where you found

Rick Lucas."

Before they could say a word, Zack had slipped away. They were left alone, in semi-darkness. The moon, far from illuminating the beach, merely cast shadows over it, which grew into creepy, unnatural shapes as their imaginations took hold. Ben had a flashlight, but its thin, wavering beam somehow made the beach around it look darker, so he switched it off.

The only sound was a faint splashing, as waves rolled over the empty shore. The minutes passed. Neither Robyn nor Ben broke the silence. Five minutes came and went. There was no sign of Zack. Ten minutes passed. The waiting and the wondering left Robyn on edge.

Then...

"What's that?" whispered Ben suddenly. "Zack?"

But he didn't appear.

"Probably a bird," Ben said firmly, "or a bat." He sounded as if he wanted to convince himself. Fifteen minutes had passed and Zack seemed to have vanished without trace. Robyn sighed. Where was he?

Her mind began to wander, thinking of Paradise... and Flora... and the cave... Then she remembered her dream. "There's nothing to be scared of," she told herself. But visions of skulls filled her mind.

"There's no such thing as spirits," Ben said, out of the blue.

Spirits? thought Robyn. The thought hadn't even occurred to her. Ben must have been brooding on his gran's tales. "No, of course not," she said. But now the thought hung in the air between them. Almost twenty minutes had passed.

"Something's wrong!" Ben burst out. "We've got to do something!"

"What?" hissed Robyn. "Besides, Zack told us to wait here."

"Only because he didn't think he'd be more than a few minutes," Ben hissed in reply. "If he hasn't come back, it's because he's in some sort of trouble. We've got to find him."

"But this morning..." said Robyn. Ben had panicked once before and Zack had been fine.

"I don't care," said Ben. He had obviously made up his mind. "I'm going anyway, even if you don't want to."

The echo of a phrase flitted through Robyn's mind. *'You have spirit, girl!'* For a brief moment, she saw a flash of skirts and a rising gangplank. "Of course I want to," Robyn said.

They set off up the grassy path, moving slowly in the darkness. Ben put his flashlight back on to guide them, but it didn't help much and their progress was slow. They headed for the trees where Zack had gone, guiding each other under branches and over vines. As their eyes became accustomed to the dark of the forest, they saw more – shadowy images resolving into bushes and trees. Then they heard the rushing noise of water.

"The waterfall," Ben muttered. "I know where we are. If we keep going with the falls to our right, we should come to the volcano. Zack might be there, or he might have gone on to another beach."

The dark outline of the volcano loomed ahead,

towering over the trees. But as they neared it, there was a sound in the undergrowth. Robyn nearly jumped out of her skin. "Did you hear *that*?" she hissed.

"A cough?" whispered Ben, in relief. "Yes! It must be Zack." But before they could go to meet him, they saw three dark figures approaching from the opposite direction, talking quietly. Was one of them Zack? If so, who was he with?

"Who's he talking to?" breathed Robyn. "I thought we were alone."

"But none of them is Zack!" Ben sounded scared and quickly switched off his flashlight. They hid behind a rock and listened.

"I got away as soon as I could," said a voice. "So come on, where are all these bones you're so panic-stricken about?"

Robyn gave a start. The voice was familiar, but it was too dark to see the face or Ben's reaction.

"I haven't got long," the voice continued. "I'm supposed to be hosting an evening of traditional music and dance. What some people will pay to see, if you stick in the word *traditional*... but if I have to listen to another blasted steel drum, I'll... "

Robyn gasped. What was *he* doing on Skull Island?

18

WHAT'S HE DOING HERE?

Robyn and Ben could hardly believe their ears. It was Gerry Sylvester. They strained to hear what was being said. The voices were lowered, but they caught most of the conversation.

"There are dozens of bones; we come across more every day." One of the men was holding something. "There's a whole pile of them. There are skulls too."

"So?" said Gerry Sylvester.

"Well, what do we do with them? How do we know we're not violating some ancient burial ground?"

"We're not violating anything," Gerry Sylvester said firmly. "Just chuck 'em. No, hold on, we should keep them all. Yes," he said, growing enthusiastic. "We'll give them a proper home. Underground. A catacomb, where tourists can see them and marvel at the mysteries of the past. A tribute to the rich ancestry of the original islanders and their sacred burial ground."

Robyn shifted uncomfortably. She wasn't sure what was going on, but she didn't like the sound of it. "How are the negotiations going?" the first man asked.

"Very well indeed!" Gerry Sylvester replied. "The Westward Islands' government is strapped for cash. Even at the price we've offered, they're eating out of my hands, almost begging me to buy Skull Island. And everybody wins. The government gets the cash, those who can afford it will enjoy the world's first ecological theme park, the *Global Green* share price will keep on rising and that's all the more money for us."

"But what about the IGPO mob?" said the first man. "How do we avoid all the outcry about the damage caused by an invasion of tourists?"

"What outcry?" said Gerry Sylvester. "No one has heard of Skull Island outside the Westward Islands. By the time they do, we'll have the place up and running *our* way. Even if IGPO do squeal, it will be too late.

"Who will doubt *Global Green*, the corporation that puts the environment first, against a pathetic little outfit like IGPO? No one's heard of them; they don't have any publicity and no contacts in the press or the media." Gerry Sylvester was talking rapidly now.

"So, there's a problem with the turtles. I'll say it happened before we arrived. We'll be putting in lots of money for research and breeding and so on. Besides, my *friend* the Minister assures me that the government will officially authorize up to ten thousand tourists a year – provided we raise our offer. Now, would the

Westward Islands' leaders agree to that, if they thought there was a *serious* risk?" He laughed sarcastically. "You've been listening to that scare-mongering warden."

"I'm worried about him, Gerry," said a new voice. "He's been snooping around. He doesn't usually visit Skull Island that often, but in the last two weeks he's been here six or seven times at least."

"Yeah, and there were kids here too. They found Rick – even asked him where his boat was."

Gerry Sylvester snorted. "I heard. Silly idiot got lost and gashed his arm as he came out of the tunnel. Good thing he kept his head. Even got the kids to take him off the island, pretending he was faint from loss of blood or something... But never mind about him. What else have you discovered?"

"Just look at this!" said the first voice.

Silence.

Robyn and Ben waited. The three men stood in a circle and looked down at something. Like warlocks around a cauldron, thought Robyn.

"Looks like a pool of thick, black sludge doesn't it? But it's pitch – natural tar. And where there's pitch, there might be oil and who knows what other mineral resources!"

"Ssshhh. Keep it down," said the second man, sounding jumpy. But Gerry Sylvester just laughed.

"Who's going to hear us out here?" he asked.

"We must find Zack!" Ben hissed urgently in Robyn's ear. "We have to tell him what's going on."

They crept away from the rock, intending to go back

to the boat when Ben lost his footing and skidded on the stony ground.

"Who's that?" cried one of the men.

Robyn and Ben didn't wait to hear more. They ran. First one way, then the other, trying to dodge the three men. Ben doubled back as one of the men lunged for him, and darted past.

"Over here!" Ben yelled, distracting the men from Robyn as she headed into the forest. Seconds later Ben was with her, the three men hot on their heels, fighting their way through dense undergrowth and tangled creepers that reached out to snare them.

"Where are we going?" she gasped as they came out of the trees. A sandy path led to a cove below, like the one they'd landed on with Zack.

"Don't talk. Run!" panted Ben.

Out of nowhere, a sudden storm burst, drenching them with warm, driving rain. The path became slippery and they were soon soaked to the skin. Robyn's sweatshirt clung to her back. She blinked, pushing back damp strands of hair which wrapped themselves around her face. She was running as fast as she could, a pounding beat thumping through her entire body.

But the gap between them and the men was narrowing. Robyn forced her legs to go faster. It made no difference. Their pursuers were gaining on them. Ben hung back to grab her arm.

"Come... on..." he panted, pulling her along. But on the beach even Ben slowed down. "What do we now?" he groaned. The sea glinted darkly ahead of them. Behind, the men had almost caught up.

"Can't... give up... now," Robyn gasped, frantically looking around. To her right, she could just make out the outline of a cliff.

It seemed familiar... But how could it be? This was the first time she'd been to this side of the island. Thoughts raced through her mind. Suddenly it all became clear. A black pool... now the cliff... Of course! This was the island Flora had written about. Flora had been... must have been... shipwrecked here, on Skull Island!

Robyn made straight for the cliff and dived through a gap in the rocks. "Great," Ben said, following her into a cave. "Now we're in a ready-made prison."

"Flora and Harry were shipwrecked here." Ben looked blank. "You know, in the journal I was reading, they were shipwrecked here on Skull Island!" she said. "Keep going! If I'm right, there'll be a tunnel at the back of the cave!"

"And if you're wro..?" Ben was asking. Then he stopped. "Oh!" There in front of them was a small tunnel, just as Robyn had said. He scrambled through it, with Robyn close behind. "Where does it go?" Ben asked, turning on his flashlight.

"Don't know," Robyn panted, remembering with a terrible shock that Flora and Harry had been trapped inside the tunnel; that they might never have come out. But angry shouts behind them wiped everything else from her mind. Heads down, she and Ben ran, following the tunnel wherever it led, until eventually, it forked in two.

"Which way now?" Ben asked. "The left passage looks smaller... less chance of them following us. Harder for them to squeeze through."

"No!" said Robyn. "Try the *right* fork. The other one could be a dead end. That was the one Flora and Harry took," she explained as they moved off, "and I don't know if they ever found a way out."

They ran on, stooping and once or twice crawling, wherever the tunnel closed in on them. And all the time, they heard the pounding footsteps behind them; sometimes fainter, sometimes almost upon them. The tunnel seemed endless, their ragged breaths and footsteps strangely magnified.

"Where are we going?" said Robyn despairingly. "It feels as if we're running all the way around the island!" She was exhausted. She couldn't go on much longer. Suddenly she stopped. The tunnel had ended in a small, dark space.

"Where are we?" Robyn cried. "It can't be a dead end." Had all their running been in vain?

Desperately, Ben shone his flashlight around but all they could see was solid rock. The shouts of their would-be captors had faded, but that didn't mean they were safe. The men would be with them any minute. Ben waved his flashlight around again, helplessly.

"There's something on the roof!" cried Robyn.

"What?" he asked, looking at her as if she was crazy.

"Just shine your flashlight up there," she said. "Yes!" Her voice shook with relief. Above them was a wooden trap door with an iron ring attached. Ben quickly helped Robyn onto his shoulders and she stretched up as high as she could.

"Well?" said Ben impatiently, hearing the footsteps in the distance getting closer.

"Hold on," Robyn grunted. She reached for the iron ring, gave it a twist and pulled. "Got it!" The trap door fell open and a rope ladder snaked to the ground. Ben let Robyn down from his shoulders with a bump. Frantically, they climbed the ladder. Seconds later, they heard footsteps once more.

"They're here," Robyn yelled. "Quick!" She hauled the rope ladder back up and closed the trap door with a thud. Ben was almost at the top of a flight of stone steps. Robyn scrambled after him, coming out into a room with small, high windows. The windows were blocked with creepers and the flagstone floor was carpeted with weeds. Before them stood an overturned packing case. Some old drinks cans were caught in the beam of Ben's flashlight. Robyn couldn't believe it. "The mill?" she gasped, in disbelief.

Ben was equally stunned. "That means the tunnel... we've run... under the sea?!"

They paused as the truth sank in. The tunnel on Skull Island ran all the way under the sea, to come out on Paradise Island! It was incredible, but there was no time to wonder how or why. Angry voices floated up through the trap door. Robyn and Ben raced out of the mill in panic, shooting across the bridge and stumbling down the grassy slope to the beach below. As they ran, an awful thought struck Robyn. There was no road to or from the mill. The only way out was by boat – and theirs was still on Skull Island.

19

CURTIS PUBLICITY

On the beach, they saw a dark shape ahead of them. Ben's flashlight flickered for a second and went out, but they had long enough to see a motor boat beached on the sand. Without a word, Robyn and Ben heaved it into the sea and climbed aboard. Anxiously, Ben yanked the starter cord.

"Come on," he begged. "Start. Come on."

Suddenly a full-throttle chugging reverberated around the island, echoing in the silence. Robyn took a last look back at the shore as the boat roared away. She could just make out three figures standing there, powerless to stop them.

Ten minutes later, they were at Eden Beach. They dragged the boat ashore, staggering over the sand and through the gardens to Robyn's cabin.

Mrs. Curtis was just coming out of the kitchen with

a cup of coffee. "Robyn? Are you OK? What on earth's happened?"

Robyn leaned against the sofa, unable to explain fast enough. "It's Gerry Sylvester. He was on Skull Island and they were talking about tourists and we found a tunnel and..."

"ZACK!" Ben broke in suddenly. "Zack! We left him behind!"

Robyn looked at Ben in horror. She'd completely forgotten about Zack in the panic of escape.

"You left Zack on *Skull Island*?" Mrs. Curtis began. "What were you doing out there? I thought this was a boat trip. And how does Gerry come into it?"

"Zack wanted to check out something on Skull Island," said Robyn, "so we went over with him, and then we heard Gerry Sylvester talking about bringing in lots of visitors for money and..."

Mrs. Curtis looked very surprised. "That doesn't sound right. Are you sure?"

"It's true, Mrs. Curtis!" Ben insisted. "We both heard him!"

"Was this before or after you 'lost' Zack?" asked Robyn's mother.

"After," Robyn said. "But we didn't lose him exactly. He heard something and went racing off, telling us to wait by his boat, but he didn't come back."

"Racing off where?" asked Mrs. Curtis.

"We don't know," cried Ben, desperately. "Anything could have happened to him!"

"Let me get this straight. You two just took his boat and *left*? We'd better go straight back."

"Oh, we didn't take Zack's boat," said Robyn. "We took Gerry's."

"*What?*" said her mother, as the phone began to ring. She snatched it up. "Hello? Zack! Are you OK? Thank goodness! No, they're fine, they're here. Yes, just arrived... They were more worried about you! Oh...? OK, see you soon!"

"That was Zack," said Mrs. Curtis, unnecessarily. "Telling me he'd alerted the coastguard that the two of you had gone missing. As soon as he's called off the search party, he'll be here. He's fine," she reassured Ben. "And perhaps when he gets here, he'll be able to tell me exactly what's going on."

* * * * * * * * * *

Zack arrived twenty minutes later. "Am I pleased to see the two of you!" he exclaimed, bursting through the door from the veranda. "I couldn't think where you'd gone. I'm sorry I left you for so long. While I was scouting around, I checked on the turtles. Not only had some of the eggs hatched, the hatchlings had already dug themselves out of their nests."

Robyn and her mother looked blankly at him.

"I had to help them reach the sea," Zack explained. "Their nests are buried a long way up the beach, and they're especially vulnerable during their first crawl to the sea. Herons and crabs lie in wait for them. Normally, with hundreds of hatchlings there, it's fine, but this year, with so few... well, I had to stay and beat off the predators. Some islands even organize night patrols to keep an eye on them," he added.

"Really?" said Mrs. Curtis.

"But what about you two?" Zack asked, turning to Ben and Robyn. "Thank goodness you're OK. How on earth did you get back here?"

"Took Gerry's boat, apparently," said Mrs. Curtis.

"*Gerry Sylvester's*?" said Zack. "What was *he* doing on Skull Island?"

"He was talking about opening it to ten thousand tourists!" said Robyn.

"Yes, *and* moving the old bones," added Ben.

"I can't believe it!" said Mrs. Curtis, shaking her head. "You must have misunderstood. Besides, Gerry was at the Old Cotton Café..." She paused. "Well, no, actually he left before the dancing began, but I'm sure his visit to Skull Island must have been innocent. Maybe he was worried about the turtles or something."

"He wants to open Skull Island to the public!" Robyn insisted in frustration. "A sort of nature theme park." Zack stared at her in disbelief.

"Well, bringing the environment to the fore is the *Global Green* way," said Mrs. Curtis uncertainly, repeating a phrase from her brochure.

"It won't bring it to the fore. That sort of thing will destroy it completely," said Zack.

"But he couldn't do it anyway," Mrs. Curtis began. "The island isn't even his."

"But it will be," said Zack. "This is highly confidential, but the Westward Islands' government is at an advanced stage of negotiations with Gerry. He's planning to *buy* Skull Island."

114

"Oh!" Mrs. Curtis exclaimed, lost for words.

"Of course, he's promised them it will be safe in his hands," Zack went on. "He's agreed to keep tourists to a minimum number, as set by the government, and says he'll respect it as a nature reserve. I'm sure the government has no idea he's been secretly checking out his purchase. Neither did I. Ten thousand tourists? I can't believe it. Skull Island will be ruined."

"But Gerry cares about the environment," said Mrs. Curtis. "He's so enthusiastic and honest and reliable..." A trace of doubt was beginning to creep into her voice. "OK, so he's called off a few meetings and he didn't seem too eager for me to meet Zack..." she murmured to herself.

"That's not all," Ben broke in. "We heard them talking about a black pool. Something to do with oil."

Zack was looking worried. "They found the pitch lake? Well that's it. Any sign of oil and all thoughts of the environment fly out of the window. Gerry must be delighted that Skull Island's such a goldmine."

Mrs. Curtis shook her head. "I'm finding this hard to take in."

"Where was Gerry's boat?" asked Zack suddenly. "And if you two took it, why didn't I see Gerry, when I scoured the island, looking for you?"

Robyn and Ben looked at each other. There was something Zack didn't know. "There's a tunnel!" they said together.

"Where?" cried Zack.

"Running from Skull Island to Paradise," Ben told him. "All the way under the sea."

"Flora described it in her journal," Robyn joined in. "And we found it too! But we never dreamed it would come out in the old sugar mill."

"Under the *sea*? In the *mill*?" Zack sounded incredulous.

"We found a pile of litter there when we explored it before," said Ben. "But we thought it was just people picnicking."

"I'm beginning to think that Gerry Sylvester has had us all fooled," Mrs. Curtis said suddenly, flicking through a pile of papers on the table.

"So *that's* how they got onto Skull Island!" Zack said. "I *knew* there was something going on. But Skull Island's so hard to navigate. There's only one place to land, and there were never any signs of a boat."

"So maybe Rick didn't have a boat either," said Ben.

"No," Zack agreed.

"But none of this will stop Gerry Sylvester!" Robyn burst out. "What are we going to do about *him*?"

"Good point." Mrs. Curtis sat down and beckoned the others to join her. "But so far he's done nothing wrong. Well, nothing illegal. Why shouldn't he look at the island he's thinking of buying?"

"But the turtles!" said Robyn. "He disturbed them."

"You can't prove it," Mrs. Curtis said.

"Your mother's right," agreed Zack, glumly.

"But we can't just stand back and watch him destroy Skull Island," cried Ben.

"No," said Mrs. Curtis slowly. "No one can stop him from buying Skull Island, not if the government wants to sell it to him. So we have to find a way to

prevent his scheme from ever getting off the ground."
She paused for a moment, thinking.

"Gerry is a well known figure," she continued.
"Who are you to stand up against him and say that
Skull Island will be ruined by tourists? It's your word
against his, and as we all know he's very convincing.
No one will believe a pair of kids and a wildlife
warden. There's IGPO of course, but no one's heard
of them," Mrs. Curtis glanced at Zack apologetically.
"Sorry Zack, but I'd never heard of IGPO until I came
here. You're powerless against Gerry and the *Global
Green* corporation, unless..." She got up to find a pen
and paper.

"Unless we let the whole world know about Skull
Island and the turtles and its unique, unspoilt
environment *before* Gerry goes and ruins it."

"And how do we do that?" asked Zack.

"Through Curtis Publicity!" said Robyn's mother,
smiling at the three puzzled faces around her. "That's
the whole point about P.R... public relations. It's all
about telling people things they don't know. Things
they *ought* to know."

"But how?" asked Robyn, impatiently.

"Through the media – newspapers, television,
radio... even the Internet."

"But how can *you* do that?" Robyn insisted.

"That's my job," said Mrs. Curtis, with a grin. "Do
you think Gerry Sylvester would employ me if I didn't
have the right contacts?"

Robyn had never really given much thought to her
mother's job before. But she was beginning to

understand.

"Listen," said Mrs. Curtis. "This story has everything going for it. The tunnel is the starting point. It's an amazing discovery and it'll get us on the national news. That's how we introduce Skull Island. We need to highlight its ancient history and the fact that it's been uninhabited for so long, which is why there's this unique environment which has nurtured and protected all sorts of rare wildlife..."

"And the turtles," Zack interrupted.

"*Especially* the turtles," said Mrs. Curtis. "This is where the international interest comes in. Leatherback turtles are an endangered species and endangered species are a worldwide issue. We'll let everyone know that the preservation of the fragile eco-system on Skull Island *must* be protected if we want to save the turtles. That means keeping tourists OUT. I'm sure we can find some experts to back us up on that..."

"But how does this stop Gerry?" said Ben

"I see," said Robyn. "Once all the stuff about Skull Island and the endangered turtles goes public, it's going to be impossible for Gerry to open the island to even a small number of tourists without looking really stupid."

"Exactly," said her mother. "He'd ruin his reputation along with the credibility of *Global Green,* which would jeopardize his entire business empire."

It was a great plan, but would it work? Robyn yawned. It was very late.

"I had a lovely evening," said Mrs. Curtis suddenly.

"Huh?" Robyn muttered.

"You know, the dance Gerry didn't attend. I met some *very* interesting people, one of whom is a local TV producer... I'll call him first thing tomorrow, but now I think it's time for bed."

"There's one last thing," said Zack, standing up to leave. "Are you going to warn Gerry or is it all going to be a big surprise?"

Mrs. Curtis paused for a moment. "I think it's only fair to tell him that we've found out about the tunnel. I'll let him know about my big press campaign. He can hardly object, can he? After all, news about Paradise should be good for business. And it's not as if he's told me about his secret plans for Skull Island."

"But that's letting him get away with it," said Ben.

"No. We're stopping him doing something wrong. We're stopping him making a lot of money out of it. And we're preventing a disaster," said Mrs. Curtis. "That's what's important."

"Let's hope he's still stuck in the mill for the night," Ben said. "That'll serve him right!"

* * * * * * * * * *

The following evening, the four of them plus Mary sat around the TV screen in the Josephs' living room. The first item on the Westward Islands News began with a view of the ruined sugar mill.

"I'm here in Paradise," said a reporter from behind a large microphone, *"where the amazing discovery was made last night of a tunnel running under the sea to Skull Island, famous for its rich history and wildlife."*

The camera pulled back to reveal Robyn's mother.

"I have with me Mrs. Julia Curtis, spokeswoman for Gerry Sylvester, who of course, owns Paradise and the newly opened Eden resort."

A caption flashed up under Mrs. Curtis which read: JULIA CURTIS, CURTIS PUBLICITY.

"Skull Island is a Government Nature Reserve and out of bounds to everyone except wildlife wardens, without prior permission," said the reporter. *"So how was the tunnel discovered?"*

"Purely by chance," Mrs. Curtis replied briefly.

The reporter paused, waiting for more details, but Mrs. Curtis remained silent. *"Astounding!"* said the reporter, eventually. *"And it leads right here to this mill. Any ideas as to who built it?"*

"Probably the original mill owner..." Mrs. Curtis began.

"The slaves!" Ben exclaimed. He turned to Robyn. "Remember, the ones I told you about, who were sent to Skull Island and came back half crazy, ranting about bones and an underworld. I bet they were made to dig the tunnel and somehow unearthed the old graves."

"Sshhh," said Zack. "I'm trying to listen."

"Gerry Sylvester is delighted at the discovery," Mrs. Curtis was saying. *"As a committed conservationist, this tunnel link has prompted him to donate a yearly sum for the further protection of Skull Island.*

"Not only that. A small section of the tunnel on the Paradise side will be opened to the public. All profits from the venture will go to the Westward Islands'

government and their island assistance projects. Of course, the other end of the tunnel will be sealed to protect the fragile eco-system which is crucial for the survival of Skull Island and its unique wildlife."

The camera went back to the reporter. "Gerry Sylvester's concern for the environment is legendary and his newly opened Eden resort on Paradise Island is the jewel in the Global Green Corporation's crown."

The picture switched to an aerial view of Eden and then it was onto the next news item.

"Well!" said Mary. She flicked the remote control and the screen went blank.

Robyn was looking puzzled. "Is it true? Is Gerry Sylvester really going to *give* money to protect Skull Island?"

"You heard what the reporter said," replied her mother, with a wry smile.

"But what did you say to Gerry to make him agree to all that?" asked Zack.

"That's confidential," said Mrs. Curtis with a glint in her eye. "But I did mention that his conversation on the island had been overheard and he wasn't very happy about it."

The others were speechless.

"And I told him all about my plans for the press campaign," Mrs. Curtis continued. "I have a feature lined up about the turtles. Several wildlife experts are arriving tomorrow. The TV stations are all interested, so are the major newspapers, and I've already spoken to a couple of independent production companies about making a documentary on the plight of Skull Island."

20

FLORA

The day after the TV interview, Robyn went back to the museum with Ben. One question remained unanswered. What had happened to Flora and Harry? If anyone knew, it would be Cautious Benjamin.

Cautious greeted them as old friends as soon as they opened the door. "Come for more history?" he asked.

"Sort of," said Robyn and explained.

"Mr. Sylvester found the journal in the Governor's Mansion," Cautious told them. "He called in Ken Phipps to work on it, and when it was finished, Mr. Sylvester kept it for a while. Then he left it with me. I don't remember Ken saying it was unfinished." He shook his head. "Well, let's check the original."

Robyn wiped her hands on her shorts as Cautious opened a glass case and lifted the journal out. He put it in front of Robyn, who gently turned the yellowed pages. To her delight, there *were* more entries, though she took a moment to decipher Flora's writing.

The day after a night in the cave

*We are back in our camp. Such luck! As I had begun to despair of ever seeing the light of day again, Harry returned to the cave with a casket. Inside was a map. By whose hand we know not, but it revealed a means of escape in the form of a narrow tunnel, which led us to a cave overlooking **our** bay! It was quite hidden from view. The joy we felt on seeing our makeshift shelter was immense.*

According to the map, one of the pirates' tunnels goes all the way to the northern landmass, under the sea itself, surfacing in a mill of some sort. What a pity we cannot use it to leave the island, but it is clear that this is the main tunnel used by the pirates. What underhand business they are engaged upon I can only guess, but Harry says he saw many barrels containing liquor of some description. Perhaps they are transporting them from the mill.

The second day... (How vexing not to know the date!)

The raft is progressing, as are my fishing skills. No room for more, I am nearly at the end of this little book. I wrote too much in the cave when I feared our end was nigh.

The third day...

We have set sail upon our raft. The swell makes writing impossible. Onward to New Paradise.

July 29th

Harry and I made it safely to the northern landmass yesterday, to discover we had reached New Paradise itself! I am reunited with Father at last. Tonight he is holding a ball to celebrate my safe arrival.

I do hope I will have further adventures on New Paradise to relate in the future. (Yes, Biddy, I shall always crave an exciting life!) But for now this journal is drawing to a close. I write these last lines in the magnificent splendour of my new home. There is little left to say. As yet, Harry has no news of his brother, Jack Joseph. However, there are many islands surrounding New Paradise and I feel sure we shall find him some day. In the meantime, Harry is pleased to stay with us.

Robyn closed the journal contentedly. "It didn't feel finished before," she sighed. "Now it does."

"Joseph?" said Ben. "My surname! I wonder..."

"I think I know why the end of the journal was missing," Robyn mused. "If that was how Gerry found out about the tunnel in the first place, he wouldn't have wanted anyone else to know about it."

She smiled. The last mystery was solved and in a couple of hours she was going scuba diving with Ben and Zack – just time to squeeze in a quick postcard.

Dear Melissa, she thought. Wait till you hear what's happened in Paradise...